THE GAMBLING MAN

THE
GAMBLING MAN

•

Kent Conwell

AVALON BOOKS
NEW YORK

PRINTED IN THE UNITED STATES OF AMERICA
ON ACID-FREE PAPER
BY HADDON CRAFTSMEN, BLOOMSBURG, PENNSYLVANIA

To Rita. A very special person.
And to Gayle with all my love.

Chapter One

The afternoon sun slanted through the smoke-stained windows and over the batwing doors of the Bullseye Saloon. Dust motes danced in a yellow shaft of sunlight that appeared draped over the short flight of stairs to the small stage. Next to the stage, a tinny piano banged out the melancholy notes of "Sweet Betsy from Pike."

Late afternoon in the Bullseye was a slow time; that dead time when it was too late for daytime nipping and not late enough for serious drinking. Customers went home to the family, took the evening meal, and then returned for a fling at the gaming tables.

In the distance, thunder rolled across the surrounding forest.

Sleeves rolled up and his flat-brimmed hat square on his head, Mage Casebolt sat against the back wall at a solitary table, dealing cards to himself and four empty chairs to pass the time until the evening customers made their appearance.

A slender man, his fingers manipulated the cards, placing them exactly where he intended. He kept his eyes on the table, but his peripheral vision picked up the growing number of bar patrons gathering. Too many for the time of day. With a wry chuckle, he whispered to the King of Spades between his thumb and forefinger, "They took longer than most."

From time to time, his gray eyes flicked to the men at the bar, recognizing the majority to be steady customers of the Bullseye as well as prominent citizens of the small town of Denbee Creek. All at one time or another had sat in games with him.

He dealt the last card, then deftly flipped each hand in turn until he turned his own. With a satisfied shrug of his shoulders, he noted that his hand was once again the winning one.

Outside, the wind picked up, and the rumble of thunder shook the saloon. As if by signal, the shafts of sunlight faded. At that moment, the piano switched tunes to "Red River Valley."

Cocking an eyebrow at the new tune, Mage gathered, shuffled, then skilfully began dealing another hand, not hesitating even when he noticed the group of men moving resolutely in his direction.

The party of eight halted at the table.

Mage paused and looked up. "Afternoon, gentlemen." He fixed his eyes on the mayor, George Briggs. "Looking for a game?"

The men exchanged nervous glances. Briggs cleared his throat and tugged on the lapels of his coat. His fleshy neck rolled over the tight collar of his boiled shirt. "Reckon there ain't but one way to say it, Casebolt. You're leaving town."

Mage studied the men looking down at him. "Same song, second verse," he said.

"What's that?" Mayor Briggs frowned.

Mage chuckled. "Nothing, mayor. Just a little personal joke."

"We don't want no trouble, Casebolt," Joe Travis, owner of the general store, put in.

"Yeah," added Luke Jointer, livery owner. He hiked up his baggy trousers.

With a shake of his head, Mage said, "No trouble. May I ask what brought this about?" He knew, but he was determined they were going to say it. "My games are honest games."

As one, every eye in the committee shifted to the frock coat draped over the back of the chair in which Mage was seated and then to his rolled-up sleeves.

He nodded to his bare forearms. "You can see I don't have any hideouts."

Shadows deepened in the saloon as the dark clouds rolled across the small village.

His round face growing red, Briggs shook his head. "We ain't saying you're a cheat. You're just too good for us. You ain't going to get no more business here, so you might as well leave town."

Travis spoke up. "It ain't natural a man plays poker like you do." He started to say more, but a warning glance from the mayor stopped him.

Mage studied the committee. "I beg to differ, gentlemen. It isn't that I'm so good; it's just that you are so bad. You, mayor—why, you always hold your breath when you bluff." Before the mayor could reply, Mage focused on Travis. "And you, Mr. Travis. You never let well enough alone. You break up a big pair for a flush or straight. You'll never win like that."

Travis stammered.

"I don't have to cheat to win your money," Mage added before Travis could spit out a word.

His assertion incensed the group of men. Angry mutters came from the rear.

Rolling down his sleeves and nodding to the batwing doors, Mage drawled, "But, if that's how you gentlemen feel, then I'll pack my gear and saddle my pony."

Jointer, the livery owner, spoke up. "No need. Your pony is at the rail and your satchel is on the steps. We even was thoughtful enough to pack you a slab of bacon and a bag of coffee."

With a brief nod, Mage grunted. "How about a coffee-pot?"

"That too."

Deliberately taking his time, Mage slipped into his frock coat, dropped the deck of cards in his pocket, and adjusted the .44 resting on his hip. "Well, gentlemen, it doesn't look as if you've forgotten a thing."

"We ain't," Travis said.

"Besides," Jointer said. "You was always talking about California. You might say we was helping you on your way."

Mage arched a skeptical eyebrow and gave Jointer a mocking grin. "You might."

The crack of a lightning bolt punctuated his remark.

After tying his plunder behind the cantle of the saddle, Mage swung aboard his lineback dun. "Let's move out, Sam. Folks are ready to see our backside." And without a backward glance, Mage headed down the western road for Valley Springs, a busy community west of the Piney Woods. "Let's see what our luck is there."

As he passed the outskirts of town, the storm struck.

This wasn't the first town, nor, Mage figured, would it

be the last that he had been asked to leave. The first time was New Orleans where some Cajun and Creole gamblers decided his game was more slight-of-hand than skill.

After settling that misunderstanding, Mage began playing cards sans his coat and with his sleeves rolled up. But the result was the same in every town, in every community in which he played the game of poker from New Orleans to his present circumstances in the Piney Woods of east Texas.

Two months earlier, Mage stepped off a Mississippi steamer and headed for San Francisco where he planned to go into the gambling business with his two brothers, Cap and Col.

Figuring he had a couple thousand miles to cover, Mage decided to take his time, play some cards and see the country before settling down into respectability.

He hadn't seen his younger brother, Captain, in about fourteen or so years. Even more time had elapsed since he sat around the fire and lied with his older brother, Colonel.

All his life, he and his brothers had suffered their father's blind dedication to the U.S. Army in which he was a career sergeant, having been decorated for his valor in the Creek War of 1836. He was a soldier's soldier, never a pa. And despite his wife's protestations, he named his boys Colonel, Major, and Captain.

"Well, Col isn't so bad," Mage remarked one time sitting around the fireplace. "If the old man had had a fourth one, how do you think that kid would like the name Lieutenant?"

Cap laughed. "Yeah. There ain't much you can shorten Lieutenant to."

"Well, there's always Lew," Col put in.

Mage laughed. "Or Lute."

The youngest one, Cap, looked around. "You think Pa woulda kept naming them like that if he'd had five or six more?"

Mage nodded. "That old coot? You're mighty right. All the way down to Private."

Under his slicker, Mage remained relatively dry, for the thick canopy of leaves blunted the effects of the passing storm. The track Mage followed was narrow and crooked, twisting through the thick growth of giant loblolly pines and spreading oaks and maples. He figured reaching Valley Springs in a couple days.

When he pulled up to camp for the night, eyes watched from the dark depths of the forest.

Chapter Two

The last of the prairie schooners rolled off the ferry at Smith's Landing on the Neches River and proceeded along the track to where the other wagons had made camp for the night.

Bright campfires punched inviting beacons into an encroaching twilight that always comes early in the forest. "They sure be a welcome sight, don't they, Martha," Adam Reynolds said to his wife.

Martha Reynolds cast a concerned glance over her shoulder at the sleeping form of their daughter in the bed of the wagon. "I'm certain worried about Katherine, Adam. She's vomiting some."

The weariness of two months of sixteen-hour days tugged at Adam. He set his jaw and fixed his gray eyes on the distant campfires. "Don't worry, Martha. It's probably just something she ate. We'll fix the child up good and proper tonight."

"What if we can't?" She kept her eyes on her daughter.

Adam shrugged. "We should be to Valley Springs in a few days. We'll see the doctor there."

Later that night, Adam sat at the campfire with the other immigrants, warily eyeing the storm passing to the east as they planned the coming day's route and complained about the blatantly exorbitant charges levied by the ferry owner. A dollar a wagon was unconscionable enough, but three cents for each head of cattle was outrageous.

"At least, he didn't charge no two dollars a wagon like that thief back at Burr's Ferry."

In the middle of their discussion, Martha hurried to him. "Katherine's worse. She has a fever."

Dumping the remainder of his coffee on the red sand, Adam rose quickly. "We need to bathe her to get the fever down."

Behind them, a tall, bearded settler in homespun apparel rose to his feet and stretched his long arms to the heavens. "She's in the Lord's hands, brother. Leave her be. His will be done."

Adam ignored the words.

Mage rolled up in his soogan as the small fire died down to embers. He left a couple spits of bacon over the fire and the coffeepot in the coals.

He had taken care to throw his bedroll near a patch of briars within arm's length of the picket pin for Sam, his lineback dun. He pulled his blanket up around his neck and laid his .44 on his chest.

With the briars to his side, and Sam behind him, Mage could keep an eye on the other two sides. When he first heard the faint rustling in the forest, he continued sipping his coffee and stirring the fire. He kept his eyes on the small flames leaping from the burning logs. The sounds might have been an armadillo, or maybe a rabbit, or even a deer.

He was taking no chances. "Maybe" could kill a man.

He tilted the brim of his hat over his eyes, casting them in darkness so what little firelight remained would not reflect from them.

The night grew still. His pony grazed peacefully. An hour passed. Somewhere during that time, Mage drifted off into sleep.

The sudden jittering of Sam's hooves awakened him. He lay motionless, his eyes searching the forest at his feet and off to his right. The waning moon had risen, casting a bluish glow over the small clearing in which he camped.

All he heard were the sounds of the night—crickets, owls, coyotes, an occasional squeal of a rabbit.

Shadows blended into darker shadows, and then one moved on the edge of the clearing.

Mage felt his heart pounding against his chest. Slowly, he cocked the .44, and waited.

The shadow crept toward the faint embers of the fire.

Moving slowly as to make no sound, Mage eased the .44 to the edge of the blankets.

The shadow paused phantom against the dying embers.

Moments later, Mage heard faint, guttural sounds of hasty chewing and swallowing followed by the rustle of a coffeepot and the sound of liquid splashing on the ground.

Poor jasper must be desperate, Mage told himself.

Then, in a hard, low voice, he said, "Don't move an inch, mister. I got a .44 Colt pointed at you, and I'm spooky enough to blow your head clean off."

All sounds ceased. The shadow froze.

Mage continued. "I can see you by the fire. I mean you

no harm, but I ain't comfortable when a hombre comes into my camp without asking. Now, if you aren't looking for trouble, then toss a couple of them dry branches on the fire. If you don't then I'll figure you want to start shooting."

Several tense seconds passed. Then the faint thump of branches hitting coals. Moments later, a tiny flame flickered to life, revealing a grimy, bearded creature all hunkered over like a scared rabbit, staring at Mage with eyes wide as pie plates.

As the fire flared, Mage saw the man carried no weapon. His clothes were rags, his feet bare, his black face bearded.

Mage sat up, keeping the .44 trained on the cowering man. "Who are you? What's your name?"

Shivering in fear, the man stuttered out. "Th–they calls me Joe, mister."

Rising to his feet, Mage crossed the camp to the fire. He saw instantly that he was in no danger of the frail man. "You hungry, Joe?"

Despite the fear in his eyes, Joe nodded.

"Then eat. Pour some coffee in the cup." Throwing more logs on the fire, Mage squatted and studied his ravenous visitor. It was obvious the few pieces of bacon would not suffice, so he cut more.

The rail-thin old man could barely wait until the bacon was singed before gobbling it down, all the while casting wary glances at Mage.

As the starving man downed his victuals, Mage learned that Joe was a freed slave. He had been accused of shooting a white man in Natchitoches, Louisiana and escaped just before a frenzied mob came looking to hang him. He fled across the Sabine River and lived in the vast forest of east Texas, surviving off what he could steal, beg, or run down.

"I'm going on to Valley Springs tomorrow. You're welcome to ride with me. Old Sam there," Mage said, nodding to his pony, "he can carry two easy enough."

Joe shook his head emphatically. "No, sir. I thanks you, but no sir."

"You're not wanted in Texas, are you?"

Joe glanced into the darkness. "No. No, I ain't. But, I's a darky, mister. The white folks, they don't approve none of me. No, sir. I stay in the big woods where I can hide."

Mage studied the man a few seconds, then shrugged. "Have it your way." He pulled a blanket from his soogan and tossed it to the crouching man. "Take this blanket. You're welcome to sleep here tonight. I'll rustle us up a breakfast before I pull out in the morning."

Joe didn't argue.

And he was still there next morning when Mage rolled out of his soogan before sunrise.

The sun rose into a cloudless sky, promising Valley Springs a clear spring day. Walter Beauchamp, mayor of the small community and the town's only blacksmith, peered through the open front door of Webb's General Store and waved at C.A. Webb as he passed.

C.A. stepped onto the boardwalk and called out to the departing mayor, "Morning, Walt. Right nice day."

"Sure thing, C.A.," the burly blacksmith called over his shoulder. "Afraid it's going to be a mite hot though."

The blacksmith shop was next to the livery at the end of the street. Beauchamp swung open the unlocked doors and fired up the forge. He threw open the back doors to permit an uninterrupted flow of air through the shop. Even with the breeze, temperatures in the shop later that day would reach over a hundred.

He grained and watered the half-dozen cow horses in the corral, all scheduled for new shoes. Several 44-inch and

50-inch wagon wheels leaned against the wall with broken spokes or thrown tires.

As he pumped the leather bellows of the forge, he glanced out the front doors. Through the shower of sparks thrown off by the bellows, he saw three of the town's ladies marching down the middle of Main Street in his direction. Dust puffed up around the hems of their calico dresses. Each wore a sunbonnet against the early morning rays.

Beauchamp cringed inwardly. He ran thick fingers through his thinning hair. He knew the purpose of their visit, and unfortunately, he didn't have the answer they wanted.

"Good morning, mayor," Maude Webb said sweetly— too sweetly—coming to a halt at the entrance to the black-smith shop. She glanced distastefully at the coal dust covering the floor. The other two ladies, Bernice Stanley and Esther Hammonds, stopped at her heels and nodded greetings. Bernice fanned herself with a cardboard fan from church.

"Morning, Missus Webb. Ladies." Deliberately, he pumped the leather bellows. More sparks flew out.

But Maude squared her shoulders and stood her ground. "Mayor, we've come to see when the new teacher is arriving. The children need to be in school getting an education."

Beauchamp glanced down at the cheery–red coals in the forge and suppressed a grin. What Maude really meant was that being out of school, the kids were driving the parents crazier than a mule with a belly full of loco weed. As one, the parents of Valley Springs wanted their offspring back in school and out of their hair, at least for eight hours a day.

The mayor put on a solemn expression. "Yes, ma'am. And that's how the town council feels. These youngsters need to learn good. Just yesterday, we got news on the stage that the new school marm will be here in two months. She ain't finished her teacher studies at that college."

The three ladies gasped. Bernice fanned faster.

Maude pressed her fingers to her thin lips in shock, her eyes growing wide. "Why, that . . . that's almost summer."

Beauchamp shrugged. "We're doing the best we can, ladies."

"Well," Bernice said, looking at the mayor down her nose. "Your *best* doesn't seem to be good enough. We as taxpaying citizens have a right to expect our elected officials to do their jobs like they should. You don't have children at home, so you don't remember what it was like."

For at least the tenth time in the month since spinster Alwilda Red had stormed off her job and left Valley Springs without a teacher, Beauchamp was forced to listen to the ladies of the town complain about the lack of reading, writing, and arithmetic their children were receiving.

"We, that is the town council—me, your husband, C.A., Missus Webb, and Tom Sellers—asked everybody in town if they'd take over until the teacher got here, ladies. We got no takers. If I'm not mistaken, we even asked you, Bernice, and you too Maude."

Maude had a coughing seizure. Finally, she managed to explain. "I've been in a delicate condition, mayor. I've had a bad case of chills and the languishment that Dr. Shelby can't cure." She sighed to emphasize the seriousness of her special ailments.

Bernice's fan was a blur. Before she could blurt out her excuse, the mayor continued. "Well, kids is kids. They are all going to get a little wild every once in a while. Why don't you have your husbands put them to work. Been my experience tired youngsters don't have the energy to go get themselves in trouble."

With just the right amount of displeasure edging her words ever so slightly for the benefit of her friends, but not so much as to offend the mayor, Maude said, "Well, I guess you're doing the best you can, Walt. I—" She wanted to say more, but decided against it.

He nodded courteously. "Thank you, Maude. I sure am."

After the ladies left, Beauchamp stepped to his back door and whistled across the corral at Tom Sellers, who owned the livery. "Let's meet at the saloon at noon. I'll get C.A. We got business to discuss."

Sellers rolled his eyes. "The women again?"

Beauchamp held up his hands as if to say, what else. "Yeah, the women again."

Chapter Three

Over a noon meal of cold cuts, cheese, pickles, onions and bread at the saloon, the mayor, storekeeper and livery owner met. "Your kids is up and grown, Walt," C.A. Webb said. "Our two are driving my wife daft. Summer's bad enough trying to find something to keep them busy. Tack on a couple months or so during the spring, and it makes for a mighty long year."

Tom Sellers agreed. "I tried working mine at the livery, but he does more damage than he does good."

Walt Beauchamp arched an eyebrow. "Well, break his blasted neck."

Sellers took a sip of beer. "My wife would break mine then. I tell you, boys. This situation could turn ugly real fast."

"You don't have to tell me," Webb replied. "I dread going home at night for the fuss my wife makes about it."

"Well, we got to do something," the mayor said. "If we go another two months without a school teacher, the town is going to tar and feather us."

"So, what do we do?" Webb asked.

The three men stared at each other glumly.

Finally, Sellers broke the silence. "I don't know about you two, but I'm ready to grab the first warm body that comes through town and stick them in there."

The mayor looked at Sellers in disbelief. "You can't do something like that. Why, it's illegal, ain't it?"

Webb liked the idea. "So what? Trump up some charge. The sheriff's got two boys, wild heathens. A couple days ago, he was threatening to drown them both, especially the older one—the one that busted a wagon wheel trying to run over a chicken. The sheriff will be tickled pink to go along with us on anything we suggest if it means getting his youngsters out of his hair."

Shaking his head slowly, Beauchamp frowned. "I don't know, boys. It don't seem right to grab some unsuspecting soul and saddle them with our children like that."

Sellers snorted. "Who would you saddle them with, you or some stranger?"

The mayor grew sober. "We forgot about Rachel Jo."

"Rachel Jo Perkins," Webb said. "Why is it of all the towns in the west, ours is the only one with a woman sticking her nose in politics?"

"Well, she does run the post office," Sellers said lamely. "And she is the one who helped us bring in that last teacher."

The three men stared at each other morosely. More than once, Rachel Jo Perkins had created a stir over some of the shenanigans the town fathers had tried to pull. Like the time she insisted all council meetings be held in public, or the time they tried to block the sale of a small farm south of town to a black family, or when they tried to award the school teacher's position a princely salary of twenty dollars a month to Webb's nephew, who was fourteen when he finally graduated from the second grade.

Beauchamp studied his two compadres. "She finds out about this, she'll pitch a fit."

"Let her," Sellers said. "We asked her to take the job, but she refused. I don't see how she's got any say in it at all."

Mage deliberately fried up the remainder of his bacon, knowing he could pick up more grub in Valley Springs the next day. He ate a couple slices and downed a cup of coffee, leaving the rest of the breakfast for Joe.

By the time he saddled Sam and tied his plunder on the back of the cantle, Joe had cleaned up every speck of bacon and swallowed every drop of coffee.

Mage put the skillet and pot away. He looked over the saddle at Joe who was still squatting by the dying fire. "You're still welcome to ride along with me."

Joe rose quickly and shook his head. He held out the blanket.

"No. You keep it." Mage grimaced at the sight of the ragged and shoeless man before him. "You got a knife or anything?"

Once again, Joe shook his head and dropped his gaze to the ground.

Mage looked around the forest at the towering pines and giant oaks. It didn't make any sense to him, but he felt an obligation to the ragged man. He didn't know why, but he did.

Besides, he could buy more supplies when he reached town.

He untied his satchel and fumbled through it, frowning when he realized his send-off committee back in Denbee had not packed his other change of clothes. With a sigh, he pulled out a push dagger that had come from an unlucky card cheat back in Lawtell.

The unique knife had two holes in the guard for fingers and a shorter handle designed to fit into the heel of the hand, allowing leverage so the combatant could push the knife instead of cutting or stabbing. He had planned on keeping the dagger as a curiosity, but he figured Joe had more of a need for it than he. "Here. You need something to take care of yourself." The gift surprised Joe.

As Mage rode out, he glanced back to see Joe standing in the middle of the track looking after him, the blanket draped over his shoulder and the knife clutched to his chest with both hands.

Turning back to the trail ahead, he pulled out a bag of Bull Durham and deftly rolled a cigarette. His gray eyes searched the forest around him. Despite reports of Comanche and Apache leaving Indian Territory to the north and roaming through central Texas, Mage's thoughts went back to Joe.

He looked back, but Joe had vanished.

With a sigh, he settled into the saddle and gave his pony a squeeze. "Let's go, Sam. We're wasting time."

Mage knew what it felt like to be out in the world with no friends, no home, and no food. The last time he had seen his younger brother, Cap, was in 1861, just after word came that their pa had been killed in an accident at a Union bivouac somewhere in Tennessee. Their older brother, Col, had pulled out the year before, swearing to join the Army and find their father.

Mage and Cap refused to accompany Col. "He weren't

no pa to me. I never saw him more than two days at a time," Cap said, setting his jaw and defying his older brother to dispute his claim. "You go look for him. I'm staying right here."

And so Col rode out, leaving his two younger brothers behind.

Chances are the two boys would have remained right there on the farm had it not been for well-meaning neighbors and the local law who wanted to split the boys up and put them in foster homes.

During the boys' effort to escape, they were separated. Mage ended up with a patent medicine show under the guidance of Dr. Horatio Aloysius Bender, traipsing about the country and selling everything from snake oil to skillets.

A Renaissance man, though certainly not of the magnitude of a Leonardo da Vinci or Christopher Columbus, Doc Bender turned out to be the father Mage never had. For the next ten years, as they leisurely journeyed from Georgia to Mississippi to Texas and up to Tennessee, Mage absorbed the old man's instruction like a sponge. He pored through the classics, developed a working familiarity with French, Latin, and Spanish, and acquired a deep appreciation for the art of the world.

The old snake-oil salesman, Doc Bender, sported a white mustache and goatee, looking every inch the part of the aristocratic southern gentleman in his black claw-hammer coat, ruffled shirt, and gray trousers. "When I die, boy," he told Mage on more than one occasion, "dress me in these duds and burn me with my wagon." He laid his hand on the side of the green and yellow Studebaker wagon. "It's as much a part of me as my right hand."

Doc Bender could flim-flam with the best of them, but he remained honest, and taught Mage to do the same. Mage became adept at cards, the shell game, and concocting medicines as well as developing a skill for handguns and fists. He had a natural gift to calm hot tempers and soothe injured feelings.

On occasion, however, community outrage could not be tempered, neither by Doc Bender's powers of persuasion nor Mage's entreaties. That's when it was left up to the younger man to handle the problems with guns or fists.

But, the life of a snake-oil salesman gave him freedom, excitement, coins in his pocket, and the opportunity to meet young ladies of every walk.

Doc Bender died in his sleep in a peaceful little glen near Cairo, Illinois in 1870. With tears in his eyes, Mage laid the old man—dressed in his Sunday best—in the back of the wagon, turned the mules loose, and true to the old gentleman's request, put the torch to him and the wagon.

That afternoon, Mage stepped aboard the New Orleans Star, one of the newest side-wheelers on the river. She was twenty-eight feet wide, one hundred and fifty feet long, and powered by five-foot stroke Clinton engines driven by coal-powered boilers that pushed the riverboat upstream at four miles-per-hour.

After he deposited his few possessions in his room, he headed for the poker tables where, over the next few months, he built a reputation as an amiable gambler who ran a honest game.

At Christmas of '74, a year-old letter from his younger brother ran him down in St. Louis. Cap had finally got together with their older brother, Col, and the two were planning to open a gambling house in San Francisco. They wanted Mage to join them. Immediately, he posted a reply, telling his brothers he was on the way.

When he reached New Orleans, he stepped off the riverboat for the last time.

*   *   *

The small wagon train crawled through the thick forests of east Texas. To the inexperienced, the shadowy glens and baygalls smothered with muscadine vines and wild azaleas appeared cool and inviting. The reality was just the opposite. The thick canopy of leaves held in the moisture and heat rising from the soft soil, creating a suffocating humidity that clung to a body like wet clothing. Walking even became a chore, for each breath drawn seemed to be filled with hot water.

Adam Reynolds trudged beside his mules, cursing them, wishing they were oxen. Oxen were slower, but not as much trouble as the mules. Even though mules could handle the heat better, oxen could feed on natural vegetation. Adam could have saved money on grain. He shook his head. The whole idea of heading to Oregon was foolish. He should have seen what was ahead. From the beginning, there had been one problem after another.

Had he known better, he would never have joined a wagon train with Conestogas. And he would have opted for oxen. And he would have packed in more medicines. And he would have taken a northern trail. But, that was all hindsight. He had no choice now. For better or worse, he had to go forward.

His wife peered out the wagon. When he looked up at her she shook her head, then disappeared back inside to tend their ailing daughter.

Suddenly, the wagon in front of him clattered to a halt. Adam tugged on the reins, pulling his team to a halt. "Whoa, boys. Whoa." He wrapped the reins around the brake and hurried forward.

He cursed when he saw the Conestoga stuck in the narrow stream. It was the second time that day they had to stop for a bogged Conestoga. The huge wagons were too big for the journey to Oregon.

Half the size of the Conestogas, prairie schooners could make half again as many miles as the larger wagon. And they didn't bog down in every creek.

He muttered a curse as he waded into the creek and threw his shoulder into the tailgate of the Conestoga along with the other men in the train. Others grabbed the oaken spokes of the wheels.

The driver climbed into the seat and gave a shout. "He-yyyeah!" He popped the reins and the mules threw their shoulders into the hames, straining to move the heavy wagon.

Clenching his teeth, Adam groaned to break the wagon free of the sucking mud. Mules grunted and squealed; men cursed. Abruptly, the heavy wagon lurched free.

As one, the exhausted and muddy immigrants cheered, but a sudden, sharp crack silenced them. In the next second, the iron tire wobbled off the rear wheel and rolled into a patch of wild huckleberries along the side of the track. The felly rim, that oaken hoop to which the spokes were attached and on which the iron tire was shrunk, had shattered.

The Conestoga skidded to the ground, digging the rear hub into soft soil. A burst of curses broke the humid silence of the forest.

In the rear of Adam's prairie schooner, his wife gently bathed their daughter's face and prayed.

Chapter Four

Mage rode out of the vast forest of longleaf pine and shagbark hickory that cloaked the eastern portion of Texas. Ahead lay the great rolling plains that spread farther than the eye could see.

He reined up. "Hold on, Sam," he said, staring in awe at the lush, green prairie dotted with patches of vibrant blue-bonnets and bright red Indian Paint. He drew a deep breath and gazed over the amazing panorama before him.

Vast and open, the prairie filled him with a sense of unfettered freedom, a far cry from his experience in Missouri when the tornado trapped him for two days in a devastated dry goods store. Even today, close quarters made him nervous.

Mage removed his hat and drew the sleeve of his coat across his forehead. He could see why so many adventuresome men loaded up their goods and family, painted GTT—Gone To Texas—on their doors, and set out for the state. It was a great, sprawling land, and it projected a sense of intimidation and fascination.

Texas was like a selfish mistress, clutching men's hearts and drawing them inexorably into her bosom, sometimes allowing them to sample her favors, other times denying them cruelly.

With a click of his tongue, Mage sent Sam along the faint trail wending across the rolling hills. Out on the plains, Mage became more alert for renegade Indians.

Renegade. And who could blame them?

Who hadn't heard of the government's attempt to corral the Indian in a forsaken piece of nowhere called Indian Territory? And who could find fault with the angry young warriors for rebelling against such constraints—living in an area one-tenth the size they had once inhabited and holding not enough game to sustain life?

In the distance, Mage caught movement on the horizon. He pulled up and studied the object, realizing moments later it was simply a deer. He reached for the Winchester in the boot, hesitated, then drew his hand away. By tomorrow evening, he would be in Valley Springs. No sense in wasting all that meat.

That night, the soft lowing of cattle awakened him. He lay motionless at the base of a knoll, trying to pinpoint the direction from which the sound came. He decided the cattle were on the far side of the rolling knoll at which he had camped.

Silently, sixgun in hand, he crawled to the crest of the slight hill. Some distance across the prairie, fifteen or twenty head of cattle drifted slowly to the east, pushed by a handful of cowpokes.

Instinctively, Mage lowered his head. No one pushed cattle at night except rustlers. And there were too many for one man to handle. The smartest move was to wait and watch. When they were beyond hearing, then he could saddle up and push on west a few miles.

An hour before sundown next day, he rode into Valley Springs, a small, bustling town on the main road from Shreveport to Houston. A dozen or so buildings lined either side of the dusty street. Some were constructed of hewn logs, others of canvas with a false front, and still others of clapboard hauled in from Fort Worth, Dallas, or Houston.

There was the usual assortment of businesses—dry goods, two general stores, three saloons, the sheriff's office, two hotels, one boardinghouse, a livery, a blacksmith, and a smattering of other small establishments. A wooden boardwalk ran along either side of the street. Next to the boardwalk was a hitching rail to which several ponies, wagons, and carriages were tied.

Mage ignored the one or two curious glances he drew as he rode down the street and stopped at the livery. After leaving Sam to be grained and watered, he crossed the street to the Excelsior Hotel.

A man never knows what the future holds. Perhaps, said a wise man, he's better off not knowing. The poet, Robert Burns, said it most plainly ninety years earlier in his *To a Mouse*. "The best laid schemes of mice and men oft go astray."

Major Casebolt was about to experience the trauma of that line of poetry.

Before going to his room after checking in, Mage purchased clothes to replace those the good citizens back in Denbee Creek had failed to pack. In a small place like Valley Springs, frock coats, vests, gray trousers, and a ruffled shirt were not common wear. It took some time for Lloyd Nickels to find the apparel in his general store. Finally, he returned from the stock room with a frown on his face. "I have everything except the shirt with ruffles, sir, but I do have a nice boiled shirt proper for Sunday church."

After a hot bath and shave, Mage made his way to the dining room of the hotel to enjoy a large steak. Then, he went next door to the Happy Times Saloon for a drink of bourbon and a poker game.

When he pushed through the batwing doors, he suppressed a grin when he spotted three poker games in progress. He headed for the bar.

Across the saloon, C.A. Webb leaned across the table and whispered to Tom Sellers. "Who's that fancy dressed jasper bellying up to the bar?"

"Beats me."

They looked on curiously as Mage sipped his bourbon and then idly wandered about the saloon, pausing at each of the poker tables.

"Looks like a gambler to me."

Sellers nodded. "He sure ain't no cowpoke."

At that moment, half-a-dozen laughing, rowdy cowpokes came stomping through the door and headed directly for the bar. "Whiskey, bartender," one shouted across the room. "We got an almighty thirst."

"Circle L boys," Sellers whispered. "That's trouble. You best get the sheriff."

Webb gulped down the last of the bourbon, nodded, and scurried out the back door.

Mage grinned at the boisterousness of the roughhousing cowboys. He turned his attention back to a poker game as the dealer laid out the next hand.

A commotion at the bar caused him to look around. The

bartender appeared to be entreating the cowpokes to calm their rowdiness. They ignored him.

One of the cowpokes glanced around and spotted Mage looking at them. He was a squat, broad-shouldered hombre with a grizzled black beard and flattened nose. His eyes were narrow-set. He glared at Mage who grinned, nodded, and turned back to the poker game before him.

Moments later, he heard a shout, but paid no attention, figuring it was the cowboys rousting each other. Then a hand shoved him, causing Mage to stumble backward a couple steps before catching himself.

It was the cowpoke with the narrow-set eyes. He leaned forward unsteadily, glowering at Mage. "Who the blazes you looking at, fancy pants," he said. His eyes were bloodshot, and his breath reeked of bad whiskey.

Mage smiled amicably. "No one in particular, friend. Just curious about the commotion."

One of the cowpoke's compadres grabbed him by the arm. "Come on back, Luke. He didn't mean nothing by it."

Luke swatted the hand away. "I don't like him. I don't like the way he dresses. I don't like the way he talks."

The men at the poker table had forgotten all about the game. They stared up at Luke.

Mage watched the drunken man carefully. He'd dealt with his fill of drunks during the years on the road with Doc Bender. Usually, he could bring the confrontation to a peaceful close. "Well, friend. If I upset you so much, I'll take my leave."

He started to turn away, but Luke grabbed his arm. His thick fingers dug into Mage's bicep. "You ain't going nowhere 'til I say so, fancy pants. You hear me?"

Still holding his half-finished drink in his left hand, Mage faced the growling cowpoke. His voice dropped. "Or what?"

Luke's eyes grew wide in surprise, then narrowed in anger. He reached for his sixgun, but Mage was too fast. In a blur, he whipped out his .44, spun it twice in a forward roll, then jabbed it in Luke's chest. Before the stunned cowpoke could react, Mage flipped the revolver back two spins, holstered it, then whipped it out and into a dizzying sidespin, ending up with the muzzle pointed up Luke's nose. "Is that what you were going to do?"

Luke gaped at him. Silence filled the saloon. Even the tinny notes of the piano went silent.

"Now, Luke, you probably think you're tough, but no one is as tough as a .44 slug." Without another word, he gulped the rest of his drink, fished a double eagle from his pocket, then in a blur, holstered his sixgun. "Watch this, Luke, and don't forget."

Mage placed the double eagle and the empty shot glass on the back of his right hand, drew a deep breath, then whipped his hand up, hurling the two objects toward the ceiling. Faster than a striking snake, he drew and fired twice, then slammed the Colt back in its holster and ducked his head against the falling shards of glass. The coin ricocheted off the ceiling and wall and landed on the floor.

Mage picked it up and held it for all to see.

In the center of the gold double eagle was a neat hole.

Mage slid it into Luke's vest. "Listen, Luke. You can't always tell a thing by the way it looks, and no one is tougher than a .44."

At that moment, Jesse Swink, the sheriff, burst in, gun in hand. "What's going on here? Who's shooting?" He spotted Luke. "Luke! You and your boys causing trouble in here again?"

Luke stammered.

Mage spoke up. "No trouble, sheriff. I was just giving Luke a shooting lesson."

There was a smattering of giggles from around the saloon.

Mage nodded to the bartender. "I'll pay for the damage to the ceiling."

The bartender shook his head. "Forget it. It was worth it." He brought out a bottle from under the counter. "How about another drink, stranger. From the good supply this time."

While Mage accepted the drink, Sellers filled the sheriff in on what had taken place. "I never seen nobody handle a gun like that Jesse, or no shooting like that either."

Chapter Five

For the next couple days, Mage enjoyed the poker games and hospitality of Valley Springs. Through the nightly games, he became fast friends with the town fathers—livery owner Tom Sellers, Mayor Walt Beauchamp, Sheriff Jesse Swink, and C.A. Webb, owner of one of the two general stores.

None of the four were truly poker players, so Mage did his best not to win too much at a sitting. He knew that eventually, as in every hamlet behind him, these four would spearhead a committee to ask him to move on. But for the time being, he enjoyed the camaraderie of the kind of folk he hoped to settle with out in California.

"What kind of business do your brothers have out there, Mage?" Webb asked casually as he looked up from his poker hand.

"Dry goods," Mage replied. There was no way he would tell them the truth, that he and his brothers were going to run a gambling house.

Mayor Beauchamp coughed and raised the bet a dollar. "You a business man?"

Mage called the bet. "Probably not as good as C.A. here, but I get by."

The flattery had its desired effect. Webb shrugged. "Shucks," he said. "Just hard work, is all."

"No," Mage replied. "Man's got to have brains too. Got to know what people want." He shook his head and laid down the winning hand. "Takes a special type of hombre to run a successful business."

Webb grinned and tossed in his hand, oblivious to the fact he had just lost five dollars. "Well, it's right decent of you to say that, Mage."

Later in the game, Swink glanced at Sellers who nodded briefly. Swink cleared his throat. "You talk like you got a heap of schooling, Mage. You go to one of them college places?"

He shook his head and drew two cards.

"But you read and cipher," Swink persisted.

Webb shot the sheriff a pained look.

"I read and cipher, Jesse. And I only went to the eighth grade."

The sheriff shrugged. "You know what I mean."

"Now, now, boys. Let's get back to the game," the mayor said. "I feel a hot streak coming on." He winked at Mage.

During the next several deals, the subject of conversation bounced around like a tumbleweed ahead of a dust storm. At first Mage was flattered at their interest in his background, but after a few hands, many of which he won, he began to wonder just why in the Sam Hill they were so inquiring. It seemed to go beyond idle curiosity.

Mayor Beauchamp caught the puzzled frown on Mage's face when Sellers asked the gambler if he'd ever read any of "that Shakespeare feller." The rotund mayor quickly changed the subject. "How's that pony of yours, Mage? A dun, isn't he?"

Sellers shot the mayor an inquisitive look. The two men locked eyes momentarily, then looked back to their cards. Sellers chimed in. "He probably needs some exercise. How long's he been in the corral now, Mage? Two days? That dun is a fine animal. Needs to stretch his legs some. That small corral of mine don't give none of them enough exercise."

Mage studied his hand, half hearing the conversation between the mayor and liveryman. He folded his hand and absently replied. "I'd planned on taking Sam out for a spell tomorrow."

Swink threw in his cards. "I fold. Tell you what, Mage. There's a right nice lake about two hours north. About the right distance to work the kinks out of that fine animal of yours. Take a noon snooze under the shade of the big cottonwoods. Get back here around three or so."

Mage frowned. "That's a far ride."

"Oh, you'll like it" Sellers added. "Right purty country up thataway. Who knows? You might like it so much you'll think twice about California."

"I doubt that," Mage said, laughing. "But, I just might take your advice and ride up there."

Webb won the pot, and Swink called it a night.

After the town fathers left Mage at the Excelsior, they ambled down the middle of the dusty street, whispering softly. "You boys convinced like me that Mage is the one for the job?" the mayor asked.

The others nodded.

"All right. Tom, you get hold of old Ernest. Tell him to meet Mage at the lake with that chestnut pony of mine. That pony is a fine match with that one of Mage's. Tell ol' Ernest he's got to keep Mage there until midnight. All night's better, but midnight'll do."

With a brief nod, Sellers headed for the livery.

The three men stood in the middle of the silent street watching after Sellers. In the hotel, the light in Mage's room went off.

Swink chuckled. "Best sleep good tonight, partner. It'll probably be the last you'll have for a couple months."

Mage rode out late next morning. The air was crisp and the sun pleasant on his shoulders. Sam enjoyed the freedom of the open road. The shortgrass prairie was lush and green. Redtail hawks glided in great circles in the brittle blue sky.

Later, as he approached the lake, Mage spotted a thin column of smoke. Drawing closer he made out two ponies, a chestnut and a sorrel. Then the rich aroma of coffee came to him on a gentle breeze.

A few minutes later, he rode up to the fire. An old man grinned toothlessly at Mage. "Light, stranger. Coffee's on, and I was just fixing to fry up some venison."

Mage dismounted. "Obliged. Nice pair of animals you have there, especially that chestnut."

"Yep. Reckon he is. Sit. The name's Ernest Reestrom."

Next day just before noon, Mage rode into Valley Springs leading the chestnut. Webb came to the door of the general store as Mage rode past. Across the street, he spotted Swink peering out the window of the sheriff's office. The two nodded to each other.

Mage had turned the chestnut into the corral then was

wiping Sam down when Sheriff Swink approached, a grim expression on his face.

"Hello, Jesse," Mage said over his shoulder. "What's going on today?"

"This is an official visit, Mage."

The chill in the sheriff's words caused Mage to pause. He looked around, puzzled. "Official?"

"Yep. Seems like there was some horse rustling last night at the Reestrom place north of here. Old Ernest lost a chestnut just like that one you brought in."

Mage studied the sheriff a moment. "You funning me, Jesse?"

"Wish I was." He shook his head. "I'm serious as death, Mage. Ernest lost a three-year-old chestnut—like that one."

For a moment, Mage was dumbfounded. Finally, he found his voice. He touched his finger to his own chest. "You don't think that I—" He pointed to the chestnut. "That I stole that horse?'

The sheriff shook his head. "Didn't say that, Mage. But I am curious about the horse. Is it yours?"

A flush of anger washed over Mage, but he quickly suppressed it. What else could he expect, a stranger in town? He fished through his vest pocket and came up with a folded slip of paper. He kept his voice level and calm. "Yeah. I bought it from this Reestrom jasper yesterday up at the lake. Here's the bill of sale."

The sheriff read the document, arched an eyebrow, and replied. "Looks legitimate to me." He gestured over his shoulder. "If you wouldn't mind, Reestrom's over in my office now. He verifies his signature, then I won't bother you again."

Mage decided right then he was ready to leave Valley Springs in his dust. And as soon as this business about the horse was settled. "Don't mind a bit, sheriff. Lead the way."

Apologetically, the sheriff said, "I hope you understand I'm just doing my duty, Mage."

Keeping the bitterness from his voice, Mage shrugged. "I understand."

When they entered the sheriff's office, Mage looked around for the old man he had met at the lake.

Sheriff Swink crossed the room to a weathered cowboy about fifty. He extended the bill of sale. "Is this your signature?"

The old cowpoke peered at the slip of paper, then glared at Mage. "No."

Mage was confused. "Who is this man, sheriff? I've never seen him before. He isn't the one I bought the horse from."

Swink grimaced. "Sure hate to hear you say that, Mage, because this hombre is Ernest Reestrom, the rancher who owns that horse you stole."

Having spotted the sheriff and Mage heading for the jail, Webb, still wearing his store apron, Mayor Beauchamp, and Sellers had hurried after them and now stood gathered just inside the front door. Webb interrupted. "I can't believe Mage would steal a horse, sheriff."

Swink shrugged and held his hands out to his side. "Here's evidence." He held up the bill of sale. "A forged bill, and he was seen leading the horse in. I got no choice." He held out his hand. "I got to have your sixgun, Mage. You're under arrest for horse stealing."

Mage's brain raced. He couldn't believe all this was happening to him. "Listen, sheriff. Let me explain. I was at the lake last night. I got there about noon and there was this old man already there with the chestnut and a sorrel."

A sudden thought struck Mage. "Wait a minute. That

chestnut couldn't have been stolen last night. He was at the lake with me and the old man who claimed he was Ernest Reestrom. The horse couldn't have been with those that got rustled. Not last night."

Reestrom coughed and shot the mayor a furtive glance. "I don't know nothing about that. All I know is that chestnut and a bunch more of my ponies was taken."

Swink arched an eyebrow. "You was out all night, Mage. What were you up to?"

He looked from one to the other of the town fathers for help, but all scowled at him. "I would've been back, but the old man took sick. Stomach cramps. I tended him 'til he was fit to ride out this morning."

The sheriff shook his head. "Ain't much of an alibi, Mage."

Slowly, Mage lowered his hand to the butt of his sixgun. His options were running out. In the few days he had been in Valley Springs, he had come to like Jesse Swink, but he wasn't about to let the sheriff slap him in jail on a rustling charge. That was tantamount to a hanging social. He froze when he heard the click of hammers behind him.

Mayor Beauchamp spoke up. "Sure saddened to see this turn of events, son. I really was coming to like you."

Swink stepped forward and slipped Mage's handgun from the holster. He gestured to a chair. "Sit down, boy. Let's get the whole story."

"There's no story except what I told you, sheriff," Mage said, sitting and facing his former poker partners. "I don't know what's going on except I paid some old man $60 for the chestnut. He claimed he was Mr. Reestrom over there. I had no reason not to believe him."

Sellers cleared his throat. In a sober voice, he remarked. "You know, sometimes they hang horse thieves."

"Or send them to Huntsville Prison for life," Mayor Beauchamp said, a little too cheerful.

"Wait a minute, Sheriff," Webb said. "We know Mage from the last few days. Ain't there something that can be done? I just can't believe he'd steal horses." Mage gave Webb a look of gratitude until the general store owner added. "He might steal some cattle, but not horses."

Swink studied Mage for several seconds. The other men stepped in closer. "Well, I don't know. There might be a way out."

Mage blinked, unable to believe his ears. A way out? Of horse stealing? He narrowed his eyes, wary of the sheriff's next words.

"Yep," the sheriff said. "There might be a way out if old Mage here is willing. Otherwise . . ." He cocked his head to one side and made a gesture with his hand of pulling a rope upward.

Something didn't fit. Mage had no idea what, but there was a piece missing. "I don't have a whole lot of choice, sheriff. I'm not too keen on the idea of stretching a rope." When he saw Sellers and the mayor grin at each other, he knew he had fallen in among thieves.

"Well, son, maybe there is a way to work around this sorry state of affairs. Now, you appear to be an educated man. You might not have gone to one of them colleges, but you know a heap of that book stuff. Ain't that right?"

For several seconds, Mage studied the sheriff, wondering just what direction the exchange was heading. "I suppose so."

A look of smug satisfaction curled the sheriff's lips. "We'll make a deal with you, son. When it's over, you ride out and all is forgotten."

"What kind of deal?" He watched the sheriff warily.

The others drew closer.

"Well, it's a long story. I ain't going to bore you with it, but what it comes down to is that we want to hire you for the next two months."

Now Mage was really confused. "Hire me? For what?"

"For a school teacher."

Chapter Six

Back to the east, just emerging from the oak and hickory forest, the small wagon train plodded along the narrow trail leading to Valley Springs. The creak of wood and the clinking of O-rings offered a counterpoint to the singing of birds across the prairie.

Choking dust billowed up around the wagons and the feet of the weary immigrants trudging beside the prairie schooners and Conestogas. At the rear of the train, Adam Reynolds kept glancing over his shoulder in the direction of his ill daughter in the bed of the wagon. He bit his lip. He was growing more and more worried.

Within the last few days, five children and two adults had taken ill, all suffering the same symptoms—vomiting and the gallops.

He muttered a silent prayer, entreating the Lord to take care of all the ill ones.

Rachel Jo Perkins was a petite young woman with black hair, a button nose, and a hair–trigger temper. Six years earlier at seventeen, she had been critically wounded when a band of renegade Comanche and Caddo murdered her family and left her for dead.

She remained in Valley Springs upon recovering, supporting herself by what work she could find, from sewing fancy dresses to shoveling out the livery. She finally went to work for Mort Ravey, the postmaster. Upon his death, a state senator enamored with her used his influence to have her appointed as post-mistress of Valley Springs.

A single, outspoken young woman, she made the town council uncomfortable on occasion for she was well aware of their quirks and weaknesses and foibles. They were basically good men, but not above succumbing to some of the frailties of man.

And now, when she spotted three of them scurrying down in the street like mice after cheese, she figured something was up. She closed and locked the door to the rear office, and hurried after them.

As she stepped through the open door, she heard the words "for a school teacher."

His mouth agape, Mage stared up at the town fathers in disbelief. He looked from one to the other while he stammered and stuttered. Finally, he managed to speak. "You old boys are joshing me. Ain't that right." A fleeting, uncertain smile played over his lips, then faded. "This is all just a big joke."

Swink shook his shaggy head. "Afraid not, boy."

"But me—a school teacher? No. Not me. You got to be out of your mind."

Rachel Jo stared at the backs of the town council and her jaw dropped open. "What's going on here?"

The four town fathers looked around. When Swink spotted her, he rolled his eyes and groaned.

"Nothing for you to concern yourself about, Rachel Jo," Mayor Beauchamp said.

"What's this about a teacher? I hadn't heard about the teacher coming in." She took a step forward.

Webb wiped his hands nervously on his apron. "It ain't nothing for you to concern yourself about, Rachel Jo. We found a jasper who can teach the kids until the new school marm gets here. That's all."

She took a step forward. "What are you talking about? What jasper?"

The men stepped aside.

Major Casebolt smiled gratefully. "I'm mighty pleased to see you, ma'am. I hope you can point out to your friends the gravity and futility of their desires."

Sellers nodded emphatically. "See there. That's the fancy kind of education talk we meant. And Mage here knows about that Shakespeare hombre and ciphering."

"And he volunteered to keep school until the new teacher gets here," Mayor Beauchamp added.

Mage interrupted. "Well, now, mayor, I didn't exactly vol—"

Rachel Jo interrupted. "I know you. I've seen you around. You're that gambler." She turned her fierce gaze on the town council. "I'm shocked, shocked. You have the gall to turn our children over to a common gambler?" She eyed Mage distastefully. "Why, no telling what kind of vermin he runs with."

Mage shifted uncomfortably in his chair. "Well, ma'am.

Vermin. I don't know as I'd go as far as to say that, but—"

She spun on her heel and stormed toward the door. "I won't have it," she said, almost shouting. "I'll call a town meeting. I'll—"

Swink boomed out. "Then you take over the school, Rachel Jo."

She froze in the open door.

Swink continued. "You go tell all the mothers whose children are driving them crazy that there ain't going to be no school to take the kids off their hands. Now, you go right ahead, but if there ain't no school, we'll make blasted sure you get the blame. The good ladies can come see you."

She remained motionless for several seconds before slowly turning to glare at the sheriff with a look so hot it would start a prairie fire. "That's blackmail."

Mage jumped in on her side. "Don't let them get away with it, ma'am."

She glared at him. "You shut up."

Swink continued in a soft, laconic tone. "Yes, ma'am. Reckon blackmail is what it is."

For long seconds the two parties stared at each other. Finally Rachel Jo turned her gaze on Mage. "I'll be watching you, gambler. You can bet on that."

With a soft groan, Mage leaned back in the chair and closed his eyes.

"Take it easy, Mage," Webb said. "It ain't so bad. Keep you busy during the day, but we'll still have our poker games at night.

"Oh, no." Rachel Jo Perkins wasn't finished. "Now, sheriff, you have to understand something. A schoolteacher has to set examples. Consequently, there will be no more poker games as long as this—this man is teaching our children. Otherwise, I'll be the one that goes to your wives."

With a collective groan, the town council closed their eyes and shook their heads.

Mage grinned. "Well, that's it then. If I don't have source of income, I can't afford to keep my room here at the hotel. I sure don't want nothing for free."

The mayor eyed him shrewdly. "Don't worry none about that. You ain't going to pay a cent. The town'll take care of it."

During the night, Mage rose several times and peered outside, toying with the idea of skipping town, but each time, he spotted shadows below. Once, about two AM, Sheriff Swink called out. "Go back to bed, Mage. You're going to need your strength in the morning."

Mage went back to bed, but he couldn't sleep. For some reason, he was nervous as a crib girl at a Ladies' Bible study.

Early next morning, there came a knock at Mage's door. It was Webb with an armload of books and supplies. He stepped inside and dropped the materials on the bed. "I figured you could probably use some of this." He pointed out the window. "Yonder's the school, down at the end of the street. The teacher rings the bell at 7:45, but Tom Sellers will ring the bell this morning since this is your first day."

"That's mighty nice of him," Mage mumbled.

Webb missed the sarcasm. "He's happy to help you out."

With a sigh of resignation, Mage buckled on his gun belt, but when he saw Webb shake his head, he unbuckled it and draped it over the foot of his bed.

The whole town turned out to watch Mage make his way up the street to the schoolhouse. A cluster of children—

small, medium, and large—stood at the base of the steps looking on.

Eyes forward, Mage looked neither left nor right, but kept his gaze on the open door to the school.

The children parted silently as he approached. Most were younger, but at the rear stood two rawboned ranch boys well over six feet wearing a sneer on their lips. Mage had seen the look enough to know it meant trouble.

The schoolroom served also as the meeting hall for the small town. It was the location of Easter pageants, Fourth of July speeches, Thanksgiving plays, and Christmas festivities. Stacked in one corner of the room was an assortment of dividers, mirrors, and canvas sets depicting various holidays.

The class itself was made up of four girls and seven boys, ranging from eight years to fourteen. Mage started off the class by having each student stand and give their name, which he jotted down on a chart.

After the last one finished, Mage drew a deep breath and turned to the blackboard, and while he jotted a problem on the board, he spoke over his shoulder, pretending he was pitching Doc Bender's snake oil to anxious customers. "Now, one skill everyone needs is arithmetic. You might call it ciphering. Whatever you call it, it's important to you."

A snort from the rear of the room caused him to look around. One of the older boys was shaking his head and rolling his eyes.

Mage glanced at the chart, then fixed his eyes on the sneering young man. "You don't think so, William?"

"It's a waste of time." He looked at his brother and the two snickered as if they'd pulled some kind of joke.

With a crooked grin, Mage said. "You boys are brothers,

so when your pa passes, you'll have the ranch. Is it a big
one?"

"None bigger," Robert, the second brother, said.

"Bunch of cows?"

The boys snickered again. "A heap of them," William
answered.

"Okay. Let me give you a problem."

With a sneer, Robert said. "Nobody gives us problems,
schoolteacher. We do the giving."

Mage held his temper. He turned to the board and jotted
some figures. "Here's the problem. Let's say you want to
sell five hundred head to a trail herd passing through. They
offer you $7.50 a head and give you $2,750."

He looked at them. "You satisfied with that?"

The boys looked at each other. Robert shrugged. "Sure.
That's what he agreed to pay."

"You're going to take $2,750 for five hundred head?"

"Yeah. That's what we agreed."

Mage glanced around the class. "What about the rest of
you? Would you take it?"

A young girl, Abby Webb, waved her hand frantically.
"No. They're cheating themselves out of a thousand dollars."

The rest of the class giggled at the two brothers whose
faces were turning red. Mage hurried to salve their feelings.
"That's why knowing figures will help. That's why we're
going to spend time on arithmetic."

The two brothers glared at him.

Somehow, Mage made it to recess where he discovered
another set of problems. The older children harassed the
younger set. Not once during the morning did he have any
free time. If he wasn't corralling the ornery Brewster brothers, William and Robert, he was helping Abby Webb put

a lens back in her glasses or daubing coal oil on Mary Jane Barton's skinned knee.

During the lunch break, he sat at his desk and watched the children gobble down their food.

It had been a long morning so far, and it looked to be an even longer afternoon.

Chapter Seven

During the last recess of the day, Mage slumped wearily in the shade of a spreading oak and watched the children scream and bounce around like Indians at a rain dance. Deliberately, he weighed the benefits of a jail cell compared to the duties of a schoolteacher.

That was when Oleola May and her best friend, Wanda Moore, sidled up to him.

"Why aren't you out playing, girls?" Mage made an effort to sound chipper, but he wasn't too successful.

"Oh, we have been, Mr. Casebolt," Oleola replied, her pigtails popping up and down as she nodded her head.

"Yes, sir," Wanda chimed in. The two girls glanced furtively over their shoulders at the other children playing tag. "But we wanted to warn you about William and Robert."

Mage glanced at the two overgrown boys who were run-

47

ning and laughing with the others. They'd been a pain in his neck all day, first with their sullen attitudes, snide remarks, and half-a-dozen sneaky spitballs. He had planned on keeping them after school a few moments for a stern talk.

"What about them?"

It was obvious the two little girls loved to gossip for they drew closer and lowered their voices even more. "Well," Oleola began. "They're why our schoolteacher, Miss Red, left Valley Springs."

"Yes," Wanda said, barging in right over Oleola's announcement. "They was always causing poor Miss Red terrible misery with their shenanigans."

Mage nodded briefly. "What do you reckon they have on their minds?"

Wanda looked up at him somberly. "The book closet."

"The what?"

"That's what they did to Miss Red," Oleola blurted out. "They locked her in the book closet and left her all night."

"Yes," Wanda whispered, her eyes wide with excitement. "People say the snakes turned her hair gray by the time she got out next morning. I never saw, but I don't believe it."

"That's what people say." Oleola said breathlessly. "And they say her skin was wrinkled like an old witch."

"They're mean, mean, terrible boys."

Mage thanked them and sent them back to play, cautioning the two little bearers of tales to tell no one of their warning.

He studied the two brothers, Robert and William Brewster. They appeared to be good boys, just boisterous and mischievous. And their size could be intimidating to some, but Mage had faced so many loud, drunken jaspers in his travels, that he never considered size except as a way to use it against his opponent.

An idea came to mind, a mite painful for at least one of the boys, but the experience might put a little salt on their tails and calm them somewhat.

While the children played, Mage went inside. He looked over the stack of items stored in one corner and pulled out a mirror, which he then hung in a back corner of the room. He moved quickly to the book closet, pulled the door half closed and peered at the mirror.

The reflection picked up the entire room from the Brewster boys' chairs to the closet door.

He stepped outside and rang the bell. Reluctantly, the children returned to class, and Mage assigned them the task of reading from a McGuffey's Reader and summarizing on paper what they had read.

Not long before the lesson was over, William Brewster raised his hand. "Mr. Casebolt. Miss Red had a history book she sometimes let me take home. Do you think I could take it home tonight?"

"Why, I don't know why not, William. What's the name of the book?"

"Ah–ah–it's called the *History of the United States*. That's what it is. The *History of the United States*. She keeps it in the book closet."

At the words, "book closet" there was a collective intake of breaths from the entire class.

Mage suppressed a grin at the transparent attempt of the boy to sucker him into the closet. He rose and opened the closet door. "I'll take a look, William." He decided to make it easier for the boy. "Why don't you come up here while I'm looking."

"Yes, sir," William chortled. "Right away."

Mage stepped inside and quickly turned to the mirror. In the reflection, the boys were rushing forward, hands pressed to their lips to stifle their giggles.

"Hurry up, boys. I might need some help in here," Mage called out, placing his hands on the door.

Just before William touched the door, Mage said, "Never mind. I can't find it." And he shoved the door open. William flattened his face on the door. He screamed and jerked his head back, smashing the back of his skull into his brother's nose.

Both boys stood helplessly, hands to their faces, blood streaming through their fingers and down their chins. Mage stepped out and feigned surprise. "What happened, boys? You run into the door or something?" He offered them a couple clean rags. In the most sympathetic voice he could muster, he said, "You best go out to the water trough and clean up. And be careful from now on. Those doors can be dangerous."

That evening, Mage had a few visitors, two of whom complimented him on the handling of the Brewster boys. Mage played dumb. "Just an accident. That's all it was, just an accident. I opened the door just as they got there."

Mayor Beauchamp shrugged. "Accident or not, you best watch out for Turk Brewster. He's the boys' growed brother. Contrary as a stepped-on rattler. Goes around looking for trouble, and if he don't find none, he makes his own."

Next morning, the class was interrupted when the Brewster brothers showed up late. Each boy sported two black eyes and a swollen nose. Behind them was an older version of the two boys. His eyes were cold, his bearded jaw rigid, his lips stretched thin. Turk Brewster, Mage guessed.

"Morning, boys." Mage said. "Reckon those noses are mighty sore this morning."

Lowering their eyes to the ground, the boys remained

silent, deferring to their older brother who stepped forward and glared at Mage. In a raspy voice, he growled, "You the schoolteacher?"

Amicably, Mage replied. "Well, partner, not really. I'm the jasper they got looking after these youngsters, but I'm no schoolteacher."

"Well, then, I reckon you're the hombre I'm looking for. I don't cotton to no one whipping up on my brothers."

Mage glanced at the two boys. They kept their eyes fixed on the ground. Behind them, the remainder of the class held their breath as they looked on with eyes wide as wagon wheels.

"Whipped up on them? Is that what you boys said?"

William shuffled his feet while Robert hunched his shoulders together. They remained silent.

Mage continued. "Truth is, one of them ran into a door, and the other banged into him."

Turk's eyes blazed. "Ain't no door can bust a jasper's nose like that. I reckon I'm going to show you what I mean."

Quickly, Mage sized up his opponent. Turk had him by twenty pounds and three inches. It appeared the mayor was right. If Turk Brewster couldn't find trouble, he'd stir up his own. "Well, I can't say I agree, but I see you've got your mind set on taking a beating."

"Why you—"

"Hold on." Mage held up his hand. "Hold on. Don't start swinging yet. Let's go outside. No sense in busting up the furniture in here."

Turk stared at Mage, perplexed at Mage's casual acceptance of his challenge. "All right, let's go so we can stop palavering and start swinging."

More than once, Mage had averted a fight by touching his opponent's sense of humor. Mage led the way outside, hoping Turk would decide to grin instead of fight. At the top of the stairs, he spoke over his shoulder. "Now you understand. We got to decide about the rules."

"Rules?" Turk grew more perplexed. A deep frown knit his forehead. "I don't fight by no rules."

"Oh, but you got to have rules." Mage glanced over his shoulder as he started down the steps. "That's the only fair way."

Turk snapped. "Well, schoolteacher, I don't fight fair." He snarled, at the same time slamming a mallet-sized fist into the back of Mage's head, sending him flying off the steps in a somersault and landing on the hardpan around the front of the school.

Mage shook his head and blinked to clear his vision. He glimpsed a boot with a wicked spur coming down at his head. He rolled to the side, at the same time, aiming a kick at the leg on which Turk balanced.

"Hey, what the—" Turk yelled and sprawled to the ground.

Mage rolled to his feet and balled his fists. Over the years with Doc Bender, he'd had his share of fights, winning most, losing some. The one advantage he had over those he fought was that he never hesitated nor paused. Doc Bender had advised him to "start swinging and never stop until one of you are down." And swing he did, like the proverbial perpetual motion machine.

As soon as Turk lumbered to his feet, Mage busted his nose with a left jab, then followed with a crossing right that slammed the grizzled cowpoke's head aside.

Mage winced. Turk's jaw was like granite, but the slender gambler stepped forward with a left hook that spun Turk's head in the opposite direction and fired a salvo of lefts and rights to the staggering cowpoke's head. His bony fists were blurs, raining blows on Turk from every direction.

Without warning, arms wrapped around his chest from behind, pinning his arms to his side. He glanced over his shoulder. William Brewster clenched his teeth as he struggled to hold Mage for his brother.

Mage jerked around in time to see a gnarled fist coming straight at his forehead. He jerked his head aside. The fist brushed his ear and smashed William Brewster on his injured nose. The young boy groaned and sagged to the ground, releasing Mage.

But by now, Turk had a second breath. Throwing his arms wide, he charged Mage, seizing him in a bear hug and slamming him to the hardpan.

Despite the exploding stars in his head, Mage rolled aside and leaped to his feet only to catch a sledgehammer fist to the side of his head. He spun to his right, fighting off the wave of blackness threatening to sweep over him. He sucked deep draughts of air into his lungs and covered his head with his arms as Turk slammed blow after blow on Mage's arms.

Turk paused, then threw a straight right. Mage ducked under it and caught the larger man with a wicked blow to the kidney. Turk grimaced and grabbed his side. Instantly, Mage stepped forward and drove a right hook into Turk's solar plexus.

A burst of air exploded from Turk's lips, and he grabbed his belly. Mage promptly slammed a knotted fist into the man's throat.

Gagging, Turk grabbed his throat with one hand, held his belly with the other, and sagged to the ground.

Mage stared down at the groaning man. Finally he looked up and fixed his eyes on Robert Brewster. "You best get your brothers home. And I want you and William here tomorrow morning on time. Or you know what you'll get if you don't show up."

Robert nodded briefly. "Y–Yes sir, Mr. Casebolt. Yes sir."

Mage shifted his gaze to the awe-struck children on the porch. "I think it's about time for recess now, children. Go play, but behave yourselves. You hear?"

As one, they all nodded.

Chapter Eight

Several of the townsfolk saw the fight. When it was over, they hurried back to their stores and shops to spread the news. Sheriff Jesse Swink hurried over to the school when he heard.

Mage was at the well washing the dust from him with his neckerchief. He had draped his frock coat over the hitching rail nearby.

"Heard I missed a good fight."

"Never seen a good fight, sheriff," Mage replied, rolling his shirtsleeves down.

"You all right?"

"Reckon so." He touched his fingers to his jaw. "Probably be a mite sore tomorrow, but it'll wear off."

"Usually does." The sheriff rolled a Bull Durham and offered the bag to Mage.

"No thanks," Mage said.

After touching a match to the cigarette, Swink took a deep drag and blew a stream of smoke into the air. "Turk's a bad one. You best keep an eye out."

"Suppose you're right, sheriff. Of course, you stop and think about it, there are a heap different ways to be bad. A jasper doesn't have to be mean to be bad."

Swink studied him a moment, puzzled. He wasn't exactly sure what Mage meant, but he had a feeling that the young gambler wasn't referring to Turk Brewster at all.

Mage stared ruefully at his torn frock coat. "Don't suppose the town fathers will buy me another one, huh?"

"C.A. will probably let you have one at cost."

"That's mighty nice of him."

The two men leaned against the hitching rail, watching the children play.

"My boys behaving themselves?"

Mage ignored the question, asking one of his own instead. "Why didn't you old boys tell me these hooligans locked the teacher in the book closet? That was a pretty lowdown, sneaky trick not to tell me."

Swink shrugged off the accusation. "Wouldn't done you no good anyway. You didn't have a choice about the job."

Mage chuckled despite himself. "Can't argue that. All I can say is that this new schoolmarm you have coming best have the temperament of a starving grizzly."

"That bad, huh?"

Mage considered the question. "Truth is, sheriff, most of the youngsters are bright and pleasant. They're just kids trying to do what kids most likely do. Schooling is contrary to their way of life. So they act up."

Swink studied him several seconds. "I think you like this school business better than you let on."

Pushing away from the hitching rail, Mage grinned.

"Don't give no odds on that, sheriff." He raised his voice and waved toward the schoolhouse. "Okay, youngsters. Back inside."

"Oh, by the way," the sheriff called after him. "Tomorrow's the day for the brush arbor."

"The what?" Mage looked around in puzzlement.

"Don't worry. Rachel Jo Perkins said she would come by tonight and tell you all about it."

Eight miles east of Valley Springs, the wagon train pulled up to camp for the night. Several more immigrants had fallen ill, all vomiting, some taking on a bluish color as their body temperature fell.

Martha Reynolds never strayed from her daughter's side. She had heard about a sickness like this when she was a child back in Illinois. The only cure was liquids, so she continued to pour soups and broths and water down her daughter even though the liquid was expelled moments later.

Later, as the men squatted around the fire, deep in hushed conversation about their situation, Adam Reynolds said, "Two more took sick today. I think we should move out tonight. It'll be hard on the animals, but we can reach Valley Springs by noon." He glanced at his wagon, his eyes filled with anguish. "I don't think Katherine can last another day. If we wait, no telling how many more will come down with this sickness."

There were a few murmurs of consent.

Adam looked at each man around the fire. "Anyone disagree?"

They looked at each other and shrugged. "I'm game," the leader, Josh Billings, said. "Thank the Lord my family ain't been touched, but whatever this sickness is, it's spreading."

* * *

Having bathed and donned fresh clothes and strapped on his gunbelt, Mage headed down to the dining room for a thick steak and hot coffee. He jerked to a halt at the top of the stairs when he spotted Rachel Jo Perkins in the lobby looking up at him.

She wore a no-nonsense linen blouse with no collar, a long black skirt cinched at the waist with a wide black belt.

For a moment, the two stared at each other, then Mage nodded and started down the stairs. "I didn't know you were down here, Rachel. Sorry if I kept you waiting."

She shook her head, her short, dark hair bobbing. Her eyes centered on the growing bruise on Mage's jaw. "You didn't, Major. I just walked in."

He smiled warmly despite the look of disapproval in her eyes at the bruises on his face. "I was just going in for some supper. Would you care to join me? We can talk over our meal."

For a moment, Rachel hesitated, a look of uncertainty on her face.

Mage insisted. "You have to eat. Besides, maybe you'll see that I'm not the terrible monster you think I am. I've been with the children two days now, and so far, I haven't corrupted any of them."

Rachel frowned. "I don't see the humor in that, Major."

Mage shivered at the chilliness in her voice. "All I meant to say was that . . . well, never mind. Look, I was planning on supper. Would you join me?"

"No, thank you. I've eaten."

"Then how about some coffee. You can fill me in on this brush arbor business."

She sniffed. "What about your supper?"

"That can wait," he replied, shrugging it off. "The way the sheriff talked, the brush arbor seems fairly important."

"All right," she said. "Just one cup."

He ushered her into the dining room and held a chair for her. He sat across the table. "Now, what do I need to know?"

"Well, the brush arbor is part of an annual pageant for the town." She paused as the waitress approached.

An older woman carrying forty extra pounds, Lodie Barnes had run the dining room for as long as anyone could remember. She hesitated when she recognized Mage. "You're the new schoolteacher, ain't you?"

"Afraid so," Mage replied, nodding.

With a grin as wide as the Sabine River, the waitress shook her head. "You sure got a job ahead of you, son. Reckon you probably need a thick steak to give you strength for tomorrow, huh?"

Mage chuckled. "Maybe later. Right now, we just want some coffee."

"Coffee it is."

"Well," Rachel Jo said stiffly. "The brush arbor is part of our Easter pageant. It's beside a small lake a mile north of town where we have sunrise services on Easter morning." She paused as if that was all he needed to know.

Mage waited. "So, you have services. Why take the kids out there?"

Rachel paused as Lodie brought their coffee. Then she explained. "Why, to rebuild any damage to the brush arbor, naturally. It's something of a holiday for the children, and it lets them see how they are helping the community. Besides" she added slyly, "it gets them out of the town's hair while they plan the pageant."

"Out of their hair? You lost me there."

She explained. "The entire town gets together at the school to plan the pageant. The preacher, Brother Richard, is in charge. He assigns responsibilities to everyone. Even the riders from the ranches take part."

"I see. What about tools for the arbor?"

"C.A. Webb provides those. There will be a wagon in front of his store in the morning. We'll load the children in the back with the tools. It doesn't take much. Axes and bow saws."

Mage blinked, wondering if he'd heard right. "We?"

"I'm going, naturally. After all, the girls must have a chaperone."

For a moment, Mage wanted to laugh, but thought better of it. "Why, I think that's an excellent idea to include the kids, Rachel. A fine idea." He sipped his coffee.

She brushed his flattery aside. "We do it every year."

He sighed. He'd made an effort to be amiable, but she wasn't having any of it. "Well, I understand about tomorrow. Besides, if I have questions, you'll be there to keep me straight." Without waiting a reply, he signaled the waitress. "Now I think I'll have me that steak. Sure you won't join me?"

Rachel stiffened, realizing she'd been summarily dismissed. She rose with a jerk. "Goodnight."

Mage smiled. "Goodnight." And thank goodness, he told himself.

While he tucked into the steak and fried potatoes, Mage worried over the mixed feelings tumbling about in his head. On the one hand, he was looking forward to the trip to the brush arbor, but on the other, he was dreading spending a whole day with Rachel Jo Perkins. She was as friendly as a she–wolf guarding her litter of pups.

After supper, Mage ambled down the street to the livery. On impulse, he saddled Sam and took the lineback dun out to stretch his legs.

Without consciously thinking of his destination, he took the north road, heading for the small lake and the brush arbor. The night air was cool on his face, and the sweet smell of grass and wildflowers filled the night.

Frisky and well rested, Sam tugged on the bit, anxious to run. Mage gave him his head, and within seconds, the large horse reached a full gallop, flying along the well-worn road, his blurred hooves biting into the ground and throwing up puffs of dust.

Mage moved with the smooth rhythm of the pony as if he were a part of the magnificent animal. For a moment, he considered just to keep riding, past the lake and on up to the Red River, but he had given his word. And if a man went back on his word, he was also denying his own integrity and honor.

Upon returning to the livery, Mage wiped Sam down and tended the animal's feet, all the while carrying on a one-sided conversation with the horse. After removing a small stone from Sam's back foot, he grained the animal and only filled the water bucket half full so Sam wouldn't drink too much.

"You take mighty good care of that horse," a voice said from the shadows beyond the glow of the bull lantern.

Mage peered into the darkness as Tom Sellers came toward him, a bit unsteady on his feet and a half-empty whiskey bottle in his hand.

"Yep. Suppose I do. This old boy's helped me out of a heap of jams since New Orleans."

"Surprised to see you back." His eyes glittering from the effects of the alcohol, Sellers studied him curiously. "Don't know that I'd come back were I in your shoes."

Mage grinned. "I thought about it, but then, I just didn't want to miss the brush arbor."

Sellers laughed at Mage's obvious sarcasm. "Reckon that's about the premier event in this town each year," He replied with sarcasm of his own as he offered Mage the bottle. "Have one. You need courage to face them kids tomorrow."

"I'll take all the courage I can get." Mage laughed and turned the bottle up.

"How did someone like you end up out here in the middle of Texas?"

"Long story. And not too interesting."

Sellers grinned crookedly and held up the bottle. "We got time."

Chapter Nine

Next morning just after eight, Mage tossed his saddle-bags under the seat of the mud wagon parked in front of the general store. Rachel arched an eyebrow. He grinned. "Like a woman's purse, I reckon."

He climbed aboard and popped the reins on four matched sorrels. Dust billowed up around the wheels as the small group rolled out of town.

Behind him in the wagon bed was a pile of tools and nine children. Mage had the two Brewster boys forking their horses. "Can't tell when we might need a couple good cowpokes on ponies," he had said. "You ride along 'side us, you hear?"

The boys, subdued from the beating their older brother, Turk, had taken the day before, nodded meekly. They had no intention of crossing Mage.

The other boys sat at the rear of the wagon, chunking rocks at rabbits and darting prairie dogs, never coming within ten feet of one of the small creatures. The girls clustered to the front, kneeling behind the seat on which Mage and Rachel perched.

All four chattered like little magpies, blurting out one question after another without giving Mage or Rachel a chance to answer.

Why is the grass green? Why is the sky blue? Do rabbits get married? Does the girl rabbit's father have to give his permission for her to marry?

Rachel did a fair job fielding the questions. She might appear standoffish with grownups, Mage decided, but she seemed to have a special rapport with children.

Oleola May, a gangly girl with bright red hair and a face full of freckles tapped Rachel on the shoulder. "Why don't Easter come on the same day each year like Christmas?"

Rachel frowned at the girl. "Why, I don't know."

Oleola cocked her head to one side. "Then who decides?"

With a sheepish grin, Rachel shook her head. "I don't know that either, honey."

"Well, then, how do we know when it is?"

Rachel glanced briefly at Mage. "I just look at the calendar. It's on there."

Oleola considered the answer. Before she could reply, Wanda Moore spoke up. "How do the calendar people know when to have Easter?" She paused and looked up at Mage. "Do you know, Mr. Casebolt?"

Mage kept his eyes on the road. "It has to do with the full moon, Wanda."

Rachel knit her brows in a frown. For some reason, she was taken aback at his ready answer.

"A full moon?" Wanda echoed.

"Yep. The first Sunday after the first full moon after March 21."

Rachel's eyes momentarily widened in surprise.

"Really?" Abby Webb exclaimed.

"Really," Mage replied, glancing around at the girls. "It started back in pagan times with a festival called Eastre. You see, the early Christians would have been put to death if they celebrated their own holy days. The pagan festival Eastre took place about the same time the Christians worshipped the resurrection, so they planned their celebration at the same time as the festival. Over the years, they slowly converted the pagans to Christianity. Some time later, I don't know when, they changed the name Eastre to Easter."

The girls were staring at him in wonder. Abby narrowed her eyes. "Did you make that story up, Mr. Casebolt?"

He chuckled. "No, ma'am, little missy. The old man who raised me told me the story, and a heap of others," he added, a wistful sigh in his voice.

"He must've sure been smart," Mary Jane Barton exclaimed.

A sad grin played over Mage's face. "That he was. That he was."

At a loss for words, Rachel stared at him. She had never expected something like this from an itinerant gambler.

Mid-morning, the small wagon train lumbered to a halt in front of the general store in Valley Springs. The store was empty.

"Don't see a soul," Josh Billings said, standing on the empty boardwalk and looking up and down the deserted street.

"Over there," Martha Reynolds exclaimed, pointing to the schoolhouse and the end of the street.

"Looks like the whole town's there," her husband muttered.

A fit of coughing seized Billings. He gagged as he fought back cramps churning his guts. "W–We'll go up there."

Within minutes, the train stopped in front of the school and Billings staggered up the stairs and burst into the packed schoolroom. "Where's the doctor?" he shouted. "We got some sick folk here."

And he started vomiting.

The brush arbor had weathered the past year in fairly good condition. A couple hours of chopping, sawing, and hauling brought them to the noon hour where they sat around Mage in the shade of the arbor and listened in awe as he told them about the travels of Marco Polo. Even the boys fell silent as they heard of the fierce hordes of Mongols encountered by the adventurer.

Matt Swink bristled. "I bet they ain't as tough as my pa."

Mage winked at Rachel. "I reckon not, son."

Robert Brewster spoke up. "You think them Mongol fellers can whip up on the Comanche?"

"I don't know about that, Robert. The Comanche is a mighty fine horseman and fighter. I'd guess it would probably be a tossup as who could whip up on who."

By mid-afternoon, the brush arbor was ready for the sunrise services for Easter Sunday and the wagon and its occupants were heading back to Valley Springs.

Still excited, the children laughed and shouted as the wagon bounced along the road. William Brewster rode a short piece ahead of the wagon.

Rachel glanced at Mage, still finding it difficult to reconcile his trade with his obvious education. "I hear you were on the way to California."

He glanced at her and nodded. "Yep. Two brothers out there. We're going into business together."

The young postmistress was beginning to wonder if she might have been completely wrong about this man. Other than his obvious skill with cards, he was nothing like most gamblers.

"Oh? What sort of business? Ranching?"

An unbidden smile played over his lips.

She stiffened. "Did I say something funny?"

His smile grew into a chuckle. "No, ma'am. It's just that when I first hit town, the town fathers asked me the same question. I told them dry goods."

"Dry goods." She arched an eyebrow. "Well, there's always a need for dry good stores. After all, people have to have clothes and such. But you don't look like a dry goods merchant."

"Oh? What do I look like?"

Her cheeks colored. "I don't know. A gambler really."

He laughed again. "Well, you're a fairly good judge of men, Rachel. The truth is, we're opening up a gambling emporium."

A puzzled frown wrinkled her forehead. "Gambling? But why did you tell the men dry goods?"

"Because," he replied. "If I told them the truth, they wouldn't have sit in a poker game with me."

She stared at him a moment, trying to understand just what he meant by the remark.

Mage continued. "I'm an excellent poker player. I don't have to cheat. I can. I know all the tricks, but I don't need to cheat."

"But why lie about the business?"

"You tell me. What's the difference in playing cards in

a saloon with a gambler, and playing cards in a gambling house run by professional gamblers? There isn't any, but they think the one is just a regular card player and the second is a cheat."

At that moment, William Brewster wheeled his pony around and raced back to the wagon. "Rider coming, Mr. Casebolt. Riding hard. It's the sheriff."

In the distance, Mage made out the sheriff leaning over his horse's neck and slapping at the animal's flanks with his hat.

Jesse Swink yanked his foam-covered horse to a sliding halt several yards from the wagon and held up his hand. "Don't come no farther," he called out. "Stop right there." He gestured to the Brewster boys on their ponies. "You kids get back to the wagon. Don't come near me."

"What's the trouble, sheriff?" Mage had a bad feeling in the pit of his stomach.

"Cholera. The whole town's infected, says Doc Shelby. A wagon train come in with a heap of sick folk. Some of them come into the schoolhouse where we was meeting. The whole town's quarantined."

Rachel gasped. "What can we do?"

"Ain't nothing, except stay out of town."

"But there must be something we can do."

Swink shook his shaggy head. "Just keep yourselves and the younkers out of town. Doc says that's best."

"How long's the quarantine?" Mage asked.

He shook his head. His eyes were hollow from worry. "Doc don't know for sure. Most everyone around come in today except Missus Barton from the Bar X." He looked directly at Mary Jane Barton. "Your pa's in town. He said for you all to go to the ranch and let'm know what's happening."

"What about the other ranches, sheriff?"

"Only four. Most of the wranglers was in town, but a couple stayed behind to look after things. You got a mind, you can warn them not to come into town."

Robert Brewster sniffled and wiped at the tears in his eyes. "What about Turk?"

The sheriff grimaced. "Sorry, boy. He's in town with us. So's your ma and pa."

Mage took over. "Robert, you and William go see the old boys at the other three ranches. Tell them what the sheriff said. We'll go on to the Bartons'. Soon as you notify the wranglers, get back over here."

William protested. "We want to stay at our place."

Firmly, Mage replied. "No. You do what I said. You're still the responsibility of the school. Your ma and pa turned you over to me today, and I'm not turning you loose to no one except them or your brother. You understand?"

For a fleeting moment, they glared at Mage, but quickly dropped their eyes when they remembered how easily the schoolteacher had taken their brother apart. "Yes, sir."

Mage turned back to the sheriff. "You want to meet out here each day, sheriff, so you can let us know what's taking place?"

A look of gratitude filled Swink's face. "Reckon I will, Mage. Me or somebody. About noon. Tell the other ranches. We'll have someone meet them on the road too. That way, ever'body knows what's taking place."

Frustration tugged at Mage, but he knew there was nothing he could do for the folks in town except take care of their children. "Tell the kids' folks not to worry, sheriff. Rachel and I will make sure they're looked after proper."

As the sheriff turned back to town, Mage spoke to the Brewster boys. "You're older than the other students.

You're going to have to be grown up. What's the fartherest ranch from here?"

Rachel answered quickly. "Circle L, the Madeley place. About ten miles south. The Edney place is west five or six. Barton's is back north, and the Brewster place is east six or so."

Mage nodded. "William, you're the oldest. Swing west around town for Edney's first and then on to Madeley's. Then hightail it back to Barton's. It'll be after dark. Robert, you give the word at your place, then back to the Bartons'. You hear?"

Robert hesitated. "Why can't William and me just stay at our place?"

Mage stared at the young man coldly. "Because your pa and ma said you were to stay with me. Now, git! Tell the ranch hands what's going on."

Their faces pale, the boys nodded. "Don't worry. You can trust us," William said.

"I'm not worried. You take care, and hurry back."

Chapter Ten

In Valley Springs, the disease spread quickly. Doc Shelby hospitalized the ill in the Excelsior Hotel, hoping to keep them fairly isolated from the remainder of the town.

The sheriff set up men at each of the roads leading into town to turn strangers away.

And then they all sat and waited.

At the Star B, Shank Hughes leaned back against the corral rails, rolling a Bull Durham and watching through narrowed eyes as Robert Brewster disappeared into the growing dusk.

Bob Dawkins, a gimp-legged wrangler, plopped down on a bench, his bad leg stiff as a board in front of him. Dawkins frowned. "Cholera! Can you beat that? And all the boys

71

in town. That leaves the work up to us. Ain't that just my luck?"

Hughes shoved his dusty hat to the back of his head. He jutted out his square chin and stroked his bearded face. "I dunno, Bob. 'Pears to me, we might have found us a bowl of plum pudding on this deal."

Dawkins frowned up at him, failing to comprehend what Hughes was talking about. "Huh? I don't see no way this can be good for us."

Wanted for stagecoach robbery and cattle rustling up north of Indian Territory, Hughes rode out of Missouri a few years earlier and vanished into the vastness of Texas where no one asked questions as long as a hombre did his job. He had maintained a low profile, but the outlaw was always on the lookout for a quick dollar. And right now, he had an idea how he could turn this cholera epidemic into greenbacks in his pocket. "Well, Dawkins," Hughes said, pushing away from the corral rails with his shoulders. "One good thing about it is that now we can welcome our-selves to a bottle of Brewster's good whiskey."

Dawkins grinned broadly and hobbled to his feet. "Yeah, Shank. That sounds fine to me."

During the night, Hughes guzzled a bottle of whiskey and made his plans. Back in Missouri, he'd run across a cholera quarantine that had lasted almost a month. With what he had in mind, all he needed was not even two weeks, and then he'd say goodbye to the heat and dust of Texas and head for Oregon and the good life.

At the Bar X, Laura Barton took the news stoically; then with Rachel's help, set about preparing supper while Mage and the boys tended the team and looked after the animals in the barn.

Later that night after William and Robert returned, Mage gathered the children into the kitchen. He sat at the table with Laura and Rachel. "No telling how long we're going to be here, but it won't be for long. Still, we got responsibilities to tend. Now, William and Robert, say each of the other ranches have two or three riders. Every couple days, we'll stop in at each of the ranches so as to pass along word what's going on here and what's going on at the other ranches." He looked at the children. "You all understand?"

They nodded.

"All right. Now, it's bedtime. Get some sleep."

He called the Brewster boys back and waited until the other children had left the kitchen. "Boys, you're the ones I got to depend on. I don't know what's going to happen down the road. Maybe nothing. Maybe a heap. And if it does, we got no one but ourselves to depend on." He glanced briefly at Rachel who was looking at him with a puzzled frown. Mage continued. "Boys, all I know is that right now, this valley is in a mighty peculiar situation, one it has never been in before. There are still Comanche and Apache out there. Rachel, Mrs. Barton, and me can't do it all. I need you boys to help. I want you out every day, keeping your eyes peeled. Don't go so far you can't get back if you need to."

The brothers exchanged a look of anticipation and excitement.

With a rueful grin, Mage added. "Now don't go getting carried away with all this hoo-ha. It's just that when you're in something like this, you need to know what the other man is up to."

Her tone edged with gentle sarcasm, Rachel said. "Like a poker game, Major?"

He grinned sheepishly. "Yep. Like a poker game."

* * *

Bob Dawkins snored loudly on his bunk, passed out from too much blended whiskey. Shank Hughes sat motionless at the sawbuck table, leaning forward in the straightback chair. He had imbibed as much as Dawkins, but he remained cold sober, his devious mind laying out plans that would put $10,000 in his pocket.

Next morning, Hughes rode out after telling Dawkins he would be back later that night.

Dawkins nodded as he squinted into the sunlight, his head pounding, his mouth dry. All he wanted to do was get back inside where it was cool, and he could sleep. "Yeah," was all he said.

It was well after dark when Hughes returned. Dawkins, who had spent the day in his bunk trying to rid himself of his hangover, saw the light go on in the main house. Through the open curtains, he saw Hughes open old man Brewster's cabinet and pull out another bottle of a whiskey. With a grunt, he rolled over and went back to sleep.

Next morning, Hughes announced that a rider from the other ranches would be riding over for a short meeting. Dawkins shrugged Hughes' words off. He still nursed a headache.

By the time the wranglers from the other ranches rode in, Dawkins' headache had passed, but as soon as he heard Hughes' idea, the headache returned in aces.

"What do you mean, take the cattle?" He looked at Hughes in disbelief.

Rolling his broad shoulders, Hughes lit a cigarette and leaned back against the clapboard wall of the bunkhouse, placing one foot on the side of the bunkhouse and balancing himself on his other leg. "I mean, steal them. Round them up and push them out of here to Fort Worth. We can have them to the rail head in less than two weeks."

Dawkins looked at the other wranglers—Mustang Bill Lewis, Lutie Cole, Slim Bachelor, and Cooter Perl. "They'll catch us before we get five miles."

Perl gave him a gap-toothed grin. "But they won't know what we're up to, Dawkins. Don't you see? We meet 'em out on the road each day, tell 'em ever'thing is just fine as a frog's hair, and watch 'em go back to town."

Dawkins frowned. "We been doing all right. Why take a chance?"

All eyes shifted to Hughes. The burly wrangler studied Dawkins a moment, then spit on the ground. "Them twenty head we got the other night is nothing."

"Yeah, but twenty here and twenty there. It puts a few greenbacks in a jasper's pockets."

Hughes shook his head. "Sometimes I think all your cups ain't in the cupboard, Dawkins. Here's our big chance. We make one big killing, and we're fine as goose down for the rest of our lives."

Bachelor tugged at his bottom lip with his thumb and forefinger. "How many head you reckon we ought to try?"

Hughes reached for the bottle of whiskey Perl was holding. He took a hard slug and dragged his hand across his lips, then handed it to Dawkins. For a moment, the old man hesitated. With a resigned shake of his head, he took the bottle. Hughes grinned. "I been figuring that. Between the four ranches, I figure there's ten, twelve thousand head. Now, I ain't talked to the old boys at the Bar X. That's where the teacher and them kids is staying during the quarantine. I figure we ought to leave the Bar X alone. We ought to be able to get a thousand head easy from the other three and get on the road fast. I reckon it'll be a spell before anyone misses one out of ten head."

Lewis and Cole nodded. "How do we go about it?" Cole asked, taking his turn with the whiskey.

"Well, even with no interference, I figure it'll take us few days to gather them. Back southwest of town is Black Draw Gully. You know where the bend is with the grass? I figure we can rope off the gully on either end and hold 'em until we're ready. They got water and graze, so they won't go nowhere."

The rustlers grinned at each other. Lewis looked around at Hughes. "How much you reckon we can get for them?"

The brawny cowpoke shrugged and replied casually. "Probably ten, eleven dollars a head. That'll give us around twenty-five hundred each." He didn't tell them that none of them were included in his final plans.

A soft chuckle spread among the men. "Yeah, but what if that teacher and them kids find out about it?"

Hughes snorted. "How? Besides, what can they do?"

"They can spread the word to the folks in town," Dawkins replied.

His eyes narrowing, Hughes said, "Not if they're all dead."

The five conspirators eyed each other nervously. Dawkins coughed.

"But, it won't be necessary," Hughes added with a thin laugh. "Besides, I heard about that cholera stuff. Makes a body weak as a newborn kitten."

Dawkins forced a grin, but, like the others, he sensed the cold edge of cruelty in Hughes' voice.

Hughes eyed Dawkins narrowly. "You still in?"

Dawkins chewed on his bottom lip. Finally, he shook his head. "Naw, Shank. Don't reckon I am. I don't want nothing to do with hurting no women and kids."

The other four stared at Hughes who was grinning crookedly at Dawkins. "Well, now, Bob. That sorta puts us in a funny spot here."

"No, it don't. You and me been partners since last fall when I rode in. You always done right by me, so I'm returning the favor." He gestured to the barn. "I'll ride out. Maybe head down to Waco or Austin. Who knows, I might pick up a trail herd to Wichita."

Hughes remained leaning against the side of the bunkhouse, his right foot still braced against the side of the clapboard structure. He nodded slowly. "You best drop by the chuckhouse and pick up some grub."

Dawkins touched a finger to the brim of his hat. "Soon as I saddle up. You take care, hear?"

"Sure. You got no need to worry."

Dawkins turned and limped toward the barn.

Before anyone could draw a breath, Hughes' hand flashed to his Colt, and he blew a hole in the middle of Dawkins' back.

The mortally wounded cowpoke stumbled forward a couple steps, caught himself, and struggled to turn back to his partner. His lips moved, but no words came out. He stared at Hughes in stunned disbelief as his legs buckled, and he sank to the ground.

Wordlessly, Hughes rolled his Colt backward into the holster and said. "I told you that you got no need to worry." He shifted his gaze to the other four. "Anyone else?"

As one, the four shook their heads.

"Fine. Now, drag him out to the ditch behind the barn. Get some shovels and cover him up. We don't need no buzzards calling attention to us. And hurry it up. We got work to do."

Chapter Eleven

At noon, Mage met Tom Sellers out on the north road. "Where's Sheriff Swink?"

Sellers removed his floppy hat and dragged his arm across his forehead. "He came down with the cholera. Sick as can be."

Mage grimaced. "What about the other folks?"

With a shake of his head, Sellers replied. "About half the town now. Them that can are tending the sick."

"How's Doc Shelby holding up?"

"Worn to a frazzle, but that old buzzard's sure got a heap of grit. He ain't going at full chisel no more, but he's going. He came up with a mixture of sugar and salts in water for them to drink. He's pouring it down them faster than they can toss it back up. He said something about dehe–, er, de–, well, de–something."

"Dehydration."

"Yeah. That's the word. I don't understand it, but that's the word."

"Means no water, Tom. You know how you feel when you sweat a heap? Get kinda weak? Well, the body needs water. Cholera makes you lose the water and all kinds of minerals in your body. You either replace 'em, or you die."

The livery owner frowned. "You sure you never went to one of them colleges?"

Mage laughed. "I'm sure. Now you git on back, and tell everyone their youngsters are doing fine. They put themselves around a large breakfast, and they're helping around the ranch to work it off."

Both men laughed.

During the ride back to the Bar X, Mage couldn't shake the nagging feeling that something was amiss. He studied the countryside around him. Nothing was out of place. The sky was blue, the grass green and lush, the bluebonnets and Indian Paint gaudy patches of color. He shifted around in his saddle, staring in the direction of Valley Springs. Nothing. Even the dust raised by Sellers' pony had settled.

The world around him was silent and serene. From time to time, the skree of a hawk or the angry chirp of a sparrow interrupted the rhythm of the clip-clopping of hooves and the squeaking of saddle leather.

Mage saw nothing to cause alarm, so why did he feel as if he was sitting on a stack of dynamite all primed to explode?

He hadn't changed his mind about pulling foot out of town when the epidemic was over, but, all things considered he told himself, Valley Springs wouldn't be a bad place to settle down and raise a family. Perhaps not as good as some but better than most, the small village was like others, filled with folks of every nature, of every temper, of every mindset.

He shoved the nagging worries to the back of his mind. "Reckon it would be mighty boring if everyone was the same, don't you think so, old boy?" He leaned forward and patted the animal's neck.

Lutie Cole and Mustang Bill Lewis returned from burying Bob Dawkins. "Deep enough so the buzzards won't mess with him," Cole replied to Shank Hughes' question.

"Good." Hughes shook his head. "Now, here's how we'll handle the job. First, you know from the visit of the Brewster boys that each ranch is expected to meet up with someone from town out on the road. That'll be me for the Star B, Lutie for the Circle L and Slim for the Triple X. Mustang Bill and Cooter can work the herd while we're gone."

Glancing at each other nervously, the four cowpokes nodded.

Slim Bachelor spoke up. "When do we start?"

Hughes snorted. "Right now—here, with the Star B herd. Bill, you and Cooter head east to Cherokee Wells. The Star B runs a couple thousand head there. Start moving some south to the Circle L. We'll be back as soon as we meet the old boys from town. I figure with the five of us, we oughta reach the Circle L herd in a couple days."

Cooter Perl tugged at an ear. "We'll throw up a heap of dust. What if someone spots it?"

"Who?" Hughes shook his head. "Ever'one's in town." He touched his finger to his broad chest. "We're all that's out here."

"Cooter's got a point, Shank," Lewis said. "What if a stranger comes through?"

With a cruel grunt, Hughes replied. "Then he don't go out."

* * *

Leaving Robert Brewster to look after the Bar X, Mage sent William east to the Star B. "Just let them know if they need extra help with the stock, to send word. We can put four or five in the saddle." He tied his saddlebags to the cantle. "I'll head over to the Triple X and then on down to the Circle L. You'll make it back by nightfall, William. I'll probably be in well after midnight. Just you boys help Rachel take care of things around here."

Later that afternoon, Mage rode up to the main house of the Triple X. He pulled up at the hitch rail and looked around. The ranch was deserted. A few horses milled about in the corral. Cattle grazed peacefully.

In the chuckhouse, the coffeepot was still warm, indicating the Triple X wranglers had recently been in and were now probably out looking after the stock.

Mage left a note offering help if the wranglers needed it and then pushed out for the Circle L.

Night had fallen when he topped a rise and looked down on the ranch. A single light punched a dim hole in the darkness down in the shallow valley. Mage rode toward it.

Pausing on the hardpan outside the bunkhouse, Mage shouted, "Hello the bunkhouse."

He waited patiently until the door opened and a scrawny, bow-legged cowpoke holding up a lantern stepped out. "Who's that?"

"Mage Casebolt. The schoolteacher. I come to see if everything's all right and to let you know to get ahold of us if you need anything."

Lutie Cole held the lantern higher and peered up at Mage, then took a step back. "Obliged. I heard about you. You ain't got the sickness?"

"No. Me and the kids were out of town. We're staying up at the Bar X. You here by yourself?"

Without thinking, Cole replied, "No. Mustang Bill Lewis is here."

Mage looked over Cole's head. "Inside?"

"Huh? Oh, well, no. He's ah, he's rode out late to check on the cows back southwest near Black Draw. Should be in anytime now."

The rich aroma of fresh coffee drifted under Mage's nostrils. "Coffee smells mighty fetching. Think you can spare a cup before I ride back?"

Cole hesitated, then hastily replied. "We got plenty. Light, and help yourself."

The six-shooter coffee was hot and strong. Mage savored the first swallow rolling down his throat and warming his belly. He couldn't help noting that Cole was a mite fidgety. He got the feeling that his host would be much more comfortable once Mage was gone. He downed the remainder of the coffee quickly, curious as to just why Cole was so restless.

Mage rode out around nine o'clock, thanking Cole and pointing his pony north. He figured he had about four hours of riding ahead.

A mile or so out, he reined up and listened. Far to the east was the sound of hoof beats. *Mustang Bill? Lutie said Bill had ridden southwest. Who else could it be?* He listened for a few more minutes until the faint sounds died away.

He wasn't the only one out late.

When Mage reached the Bar X, Rachel met him outside. He knew immediately something was wrong.

"William hasn't returned," she said, the lantern she held up reflecting the worry in her face. "He should have been back here four hours ago."

The front door opened, and Robert stepped outside. "I want to go look for him," the young man said, his eyes daring Mage to refuse.

Dismounting, Mage handed Robert the reins. "Look, boy. You can be more help to me here than out there. Get me a fresh pony while I grab a cup of coffee and put some grub in my belly. Give me five minutes. And don't forget my saddlebags."

Robert nodded, and Rachel said, "Come inside. I kept the beef stew hot."

There's an eerie vastness about the Texas prairie that fascinates certain men, those unafraid of the unknown. Overhead, a galaxy of glittering stars cast a dim glow on the prairie where a man can peer from horizon to horizon with nothing impeding his view. The incomprehensible expanse forces such a man to come to terms with his own insignificance and recognize his niche in such a world.

Finding William Brewster would be like grabbing water with your fingers. Next to impossible, but Mage had to try. The boy might have fallen from his pony; he might have run into Apache or Comanche; he might have come across a band of scavengers. A Texan wore the reality of life and death on his shoulders with the same insouciance as if he were planning on bidding for his girlfriend's box at a church box supper.

Robert selected a sound pony for Mage, a gray that maintained a smooth-running two-step across the prairie. Mage kept the animal's nose pointing southeast. Once he reached the Star B, he'd enlist the wranglers' help to search for the boy.

Sometime later, Mage glanced at the Big Dipper. From

its position facing the North Star, he guessed the time to be around four AM.

At that moment, his pony perked his ears forward.

In the distance, a horse nickered. His pony replied.

Mage reined up, shucking his Colt.

From the darkness came a faint voice. "Somebody out there?"

Mage remained silent, squinting into the night. Another whinny came from the darkness.

The voice called out again. "Hello. Is that someone?"

A grin played over Mage's face when he recognized the voice. "William?"

"Mr. Casebolt?"

"Right here. Come on in."

Moments later, a darker shadow appeared, silhouetted against the pale blue starlight illuminating the prairie.

William reined up. "Mr. Casebolt. What are you doing out here?"

"Looking for you, boy. You didn't get back when you was supposed to. Everyone was worried."

He apologized. "I didn't mean to worry no one. I rode over to our place, the Star B, but before I got there, I spotted dust a few miles on east, close to Cherokee Wells. Pa runs a heap of cattle out there."

Mage looked down into the shadows filling the boy's face. "What did you find?"

"There was three or four wranglers pushing cows to the south."

"South huh? They got a reason to, you think?"

The young man shrugged. "Don't know. I guess they was just moving them to better graze, but the truth is from what I could see, the graze around Cherokee Wells looked mighty good to me. Besides, Pa never said nothing about moving stock. At least not that I can remember."

Mage wheeled his pony. "Let's head back to the others. Tomorrow, we'll see what we can find out."

William rode up beside him. "Yes, sir."

Chapter Twelve

Mage and William reached the Bar X at breakfast. The young boy gobbled down biscuits, redeye gravy, and fried steak while Mage sat out on the porch sipping his coffee. Rachel sat beside him as he related the events of the night before.

"I don't know if what William saw means anything or not. I figured on a couple hours sleep and then I'll ride back to the Star B this morning and have a look."

"What about the rider from town, the one you're supposed to meet at noon?"

He gave her a sly grin. "I figured on you meeting him. I don't want to send one of the youngsters. They got good intentions, but I want to have the right story from town."

Rachel chuckled. "I imagine I can handle that."

"Good."

* * *

Cooter Perl threw a saddle on his pony while Slim Bachelor stomped the coals in their small fire after a hasty breakfast.

Sparks flew and swirled about his boots. "I sure wish it was more than just us holding them cows. Over four hundred head. They decide they're going somewhere, you and me ain't going to sway their minds much."

Perl tightened the cinch and dropped his stirrup. He pulled a half empty bottle of whiskey from the saddlebags. "Stop fussing like an old woman. We'll manage them ornery cows 'til the others get here. Then we'll push the herd on south."

Muttering under his breath, Bachelor reached for his saddle and blanket.

Hoofbeats echoed across the prairie. Perl dropped his hand to the butt of his sixgun, then grinned as he recognized Shank Hughes reining up in a cloud of dust. "Surprised to see you out here this early, Shank."

The lanky cowpoke remained in his saddle, scratching his bearded jaw. "I come from the Circle L. From what Lutie says, that schoolteacher was over there last night."

Perl patted the butt of his revolver. "You reckon he suspects something?"

"Lutie said he offered a hand if they needed it with the stock. I don't reckon he suspects nothing." Hughes shook his head briefly. "He probably figures he ought to keep an eye on things while that sickness is going around. We probably ain't got nothing to worry about, but just the same, keep your eyes open."

Bachelor frowned. He'd quit school in the second grade when he was thirteen, and his reasoning faculties had not improved since. "What do we say if he asks questions?"

"Just tell him we're moving the herd to Black Draw.

That's all you got to say. We're moving the herd to Black Draw. You think you can remember that?"

Bachelor heard the threat in Hughes' voice. "Yeah. Yeah, Shank. I can remember. You bet I can remember that."

Around noon, Hughes sat slumped in his saddle, watching Tom Sellers heading back to Valley Springs. A sneering grin twisted his lips. The livery owner couldn't have brought better news. Three quarters of the town had been caught up in the cholera epidemic. Four had died, and several more were critical.

He wheeled his pony about and dug his wicked spurs into the animal's flanks. Now he had some good news to pass along to Cooter and Slim. The town would give them no trouble at all.

Rachel calmly repeated the news to Laura Barton and the children. She quickly calmed their immediate fears by assuring the youngsters that none of their parents were critical.

Matt Swink wiped at the tears in his eyes. "You think Pa's going to be all right, Miss Rachel?"

She patted his hand and hugged Abby Webb to her. "It's true your pa is ill, but he's getting good care. And with the Lord's help, he'll be fine. All your folks will be," she added, doing her best to give them a reassuring smile.

Wanda Moore's brother, Maxie, spoke up. "When do you think we can go back home?"

Mrs. Barton and Rachel exchanged worried looks. "I hope it's soon, Maxie. Right now, all we can do is pray and wait."

The sun was directly overhead when Mage reined his sorrel up on a slight rise overlooking a small lake surrounded by ancient cottonwoods. As far as the eye could see, cattle dotted the green countryside around him. He'd never had much experience at estimating stock, but he guessed he was looking at a thousand or so head. Far to the south, he spotted a faint drift of dust.

He guessed the lake below to be Cherokee Wells. He rode through the cattle to the lake, admiring the fine condition of the cows. Numerous calves frolicked about, kicking up their heels.

While the grass around the lake was grazed down, there appeared to be more than sufficient graze for a considerable number of animals.

He climbed down from his horse and dropped the reins. The animal slurped noisily of the cool water. Mage squatted and studied the lake. The source of the water was on the east shore where shelves of white limestone rose several feet. Water flowed steadily from the top shelf into a bowl in the limestone, which then overflowed into the lake below.

Leading his pony around the lake, Mage leaned under one of the tiny waterfalls, soaking his head and drinking his fill of the cold, sweet water. He wiped his face with his neckerchief while he studied the lay of land around him. Why move stock from such an ideal graze? The grass looked like it could handle twice the number of animals.

Mage shook his head. Something didn't quite fit.

Far to the east, he made out the green line of the forest. He couldn't help admiring the countryside surrounding him. Good water, rich soil, lush grass. Ready to give of its fruits to the man willing to work hard. No wonder men back east dropped everything and rushed to Texas.

He turned his attention back to the barely discernible drift of dust to the south. Impulsively, he decided to follow it.

* * *

Mage rode slowly, keeping below the rolling hills. The cloud of dust grew thicker. Off to his left, the forest edged closer.

By late afternoon, he was close enough to the slowly moving herd to grow cautious. A half-mile or so to the east was the pine and hardwood forest, the periphery of which gradually extended to the west.

With a click of his tongue and the nudge of his heels, he sent his horse toward the shelter of the forest.

Mustang Bill Lewis squinted through the dust as the distant figure disappeared into the forest. Riding drag on the herd, he adjusted his neckerchief over the bridge of his nose and signaled to Shank Hughes.

The heavily built rustler wheeled about from his flanker position and rode over to Lewis.

"You see him?" Lewis said, nodding to the forest.

Hughes nodded. "Yeah."

"What do you think? Drifter?"

The Bull Durham bobbed up and down between Hughes' lips when he replied. "Probably, but we best be sure." He took a deep drag and blew the smoke into the swirling dust about them. "I'll ride over and take a look. You boys push on another mile or so."

Lewis grunted. "Whatever you say."

Hughes flipped the cigarette through the air. Sparks exploded from the burning tip when it hit the ground. "Be back directly."

He skirted the right side of the herd, using the dust as cover. When he reached the point, Hughes headed directly for the shelter of the forest which was now less than a hundred yards distant.

Hughes knew the rider was no drifter. He couldn't explain how he knew, but he had ridden on the wrong side of the law so long that he had developed a sixth sense that told him when to be on his guard. Besides, his crew was nervous enough. He'd just ride over, take care of business, and say nothing about it. What the others didn't know wouldn't hurt them, or him.

He rode a short distance into the virgin forest. Scaly-barked pines, reaching a hundred feet, poked through the canopy of leaves of the majestic oaks and giant hickory trees, some with trunks thirty feet in diameter.

The great canopy deprived the forest floor of sunlight, eliminating undergrowth, allowing an unimpeded view for a quarter of a mile in all directions.

On occasion, violent winds and stormy weather toppled a giant tree, permitting life-nurturing sunlight to reach the thick floor of pine needles and oak leaves, which in turn generated lush growths of wild azalea, huckleberries, and mounds of thorny berry briars.

Hughes located such a windfall and eased his pony inside.

Shucking his Winchester, he dismounted and found a comfortable spot at the edge of the windfall that allowed him a clear view of the forest.

Upon entering the forest, Mage turned back south, keeping well inside the tree line. He shivered. The forest was like a great cathedral, exuding the same eerie silence and darkened shadows.

Through the trees, he spotted the herd. Unsure of just what he was going to do, he urged the pony into a gentle trot. The movement of the herd made no sense to him. The grama grass over which the herd passed was green and abundant, even more luxuriant than the graze back at Cherokee Wells.

He wasn't a cattleman, but he knew enough to realize that for whatever reason the cowpokes were moving the cattle, it wasn't for new graze.

If they weren't moving the cows to new grass, then where were they driving them? He muttered to the sorrel he was riding. "What it looks like to me, fella, is that a few ornery, no good jaspers are taking advantage of a bunch of sick folks to make themselves some money."

He allowed that he might be wrong. There might be another hole of water ahead where they planned to leave the herd. He doubted it, but he'd just follow along and see.

One of the outriders took after a stray cow that headed for the forest. Mage pulled up behind a giant pine and watched as the rider expertly cut in front of the cow and drove her back to the herd.

Mage recognized the rider as the wrangler he had met the night before. Lutie Cole. A frown wrinkled his forehead. What was a Circle L rider doing pushing Star B stock?

Before he could answer his own question, a powerful blow slammed into the side of his head, and he collapsed over the neck of his horse.

Somewhere deep in the darkness engulfing Mage, he heard the boom of a rifle and felt his frightened pony leap forward. Instinctively, Mage intertwined his fingers in the flying mane of the horse as it raced through the forest.

The forest floor dropped away into a gully, then ascended sharply. The pony stumbled as it hit the shallow gulch, sending Mage tumbling to the ground.

Hughes cursed as he saw the frightened horse bolt with Mage clinging to his back. He touched off another round. A miss. "Blast," he shouted, slamming the muzzle of the Winchester into his horse's flank and charging after the runaway horse. Whoever the drifter was, Hughes couldn't afford to let him live.

The frightened sorrel angled to the right, a blur behind the distant trees. Hughes cut to intercept him.

Chapter Thirteen

Back in Valley Springs, Doc Shelby plopped down wearily in a chair in the dining room of the Excelsior Hotel and poured himself a cup of black coffee. The skin under his eyes drooped in black rings. An equally weary Tom Sellers and Mayor Beauchamp joined him.

"What do you think, Doc?"

Shelby looked at Sellers. "Truth is, I'm worried. I figured some of them should have been better by now, but that don't seem to be the case."

The mayor sipped his coffee. "Can we get some other kind of medicine?"

"What? And where? Houston is over a hundred miles. Dallas and Fort Worth half again as far." He shook his grizzled head, drained his coffee, and pushed slowly to his feet. "No, boys. We're doing all we can. We just got to keep doing it until something breaks."

"Or until we all die," Sellers mumbled.

At the Bar X, the air was filled with tension despite the efforts of Rachel Perkins and Laura Barton to reassure the children that all was well. They were all gathered on the front porch awaiting William Brewster's return from the noon meeting with the representative from Valley Springs.

A feeling of foreboding hung in the air. All morning, Rachel had fidgeted with a feeling of discomfort, and now as the tiny black dot that was William appeared far down the road, her discomfort grew.

"He sure is riding hard." Robert Brewster said.

"Maybe he's hungry," Abby Webb replied.

The other children joined in, but Rachel frowned and took a step forward, shading her eyes with her hand. William had always treated his horse well, never driving the animal hard. But now . . .

Behind him, more dots appeared.

An alarm rang in her head. Something was terribly wrong. She turned to Laura. "Let's get the children in the house."

Laura frowned, then glanced down the road at William whose figure could now be discerned leaning over the neck of his pony and flailing at the animal's flanks with the tip of the reins.

Her heart leaped into her throat when she saw the riders far behind him. She prayed they weren't whom she thought. She spun and threw out her arms. "Quick, in the house, children. Get in the house."

For a moment, the children just stared, confused.

Rachel shoved the boys toward the house. "Inside. Now. Close the shutters."

Maxie Moore looked up at her. "Why?"

She pointed down the road. "Something's wrong. Now, get in the house and close the shutters."

He did as he was told. Rachel and Laura followed, keeping the front door open for William who was now only a few hundred yards distant.

Rachel squinted beyond the young boy. She gasped and pressed her hand to her lips. "Indians," she exclaimed.

Laura gasped. "The cellar. Children—"

"No," Rachel shouted. "We fight. We can always head for the cellar."

Nodding hurriedly, Laura grabbed Robert. "Quick. The rifles. You girls get over there in the corner." She gestured to Maxie. "Cartridges are in the drawer. Give them to the girls, then grab a rifle and find a window. You girls keep the rifles loaded."

Rachel stood at the door, waving for William to hurry. As soon as he stumbled through the doorway, she slammed it behind him.

"Comanche," he gasped out.

Laura pulled him to his feet and jammed a Winchester in his hands. "Find a window."

By now, the small band of Comanche was less than a hundred yards from the ranch house. Rachel levered a cartridge in the chamber of her Winchester and laid the front sight on a Comanche warrior. Taking a deep breath, she squeezed the trigger. Despite the sting of the rifle butt slamming into her shoulder, she grinned as the Comanche somersaulted over the rump of his pony.

At her shot, the others began firing. A rattling fusillade of gunfire raked the charging war party. At the sudden barrage, the warriors swerved and circled the house, their slugs thudding harmlessly into the thick log walls and heavy shutters.

The barrage of gunfire from the house continued, too intense for the small war party to endure. Abruptly, the warriors veered away. Whooping and screaming, three headed for the barn while the other two raced for the chuck-house.

"Those blasted heathens." Laura's eyes blazed when the first traces of smoke and fire erupted from the chuckhouse. The two Comanche emerged from the building only to be met by a murderous barrage of lead slugs. One yelped and spun to the ground, grabbing his leg. The second leaped upon his pony and returned fire until the wounded Comanche could climb on his horse.

Flames leaped from the barn.

Waving their rifles over their head in defiance, the Comanche wheeled about and raced away.

For several minutes after the Comanche disappeared, Rachel heard gunshots. She frowned at Laura who wiped at the tears in her eyes with the tip of her apron. The older woman mustered a weak grin. "Looks like we might have a heap of meat to eat."

Rachel's eyes widened. "You mean—"

Laura nodded briefly. "They're killing our stock."

Shank Hughes muttered a curse as he raced after the runaway horse. While there was sparse undergrowth in the forest, at a certain distance the trees formed a curtain of tree trunks into which a horse and rider could disappear.

From time to time, Hughes caught a glimpse of the animal only to see it vanish like a wraith into the wall of trees.

Without warning, a guttural roar echoed through the forest. Hughes reined up and jammed his Winchester into his shoulder. Bear! The roar reverberated through the forest once again, and a flash of motion caught his eyes as the pony he had been chasing raced back toward him.

Eyes rolling, the bit clenched tightly in its teeth, the horse flashed past, the saddle empty.

Hughes' horse jittered about nervously. Scratching his beard, the rustler kept his eyes on the shadowy forest before him. He shook his head and wheeled his pony about. If that jasper was back in the forest, the bear was welcome to him.

The pounding in his skull awakened Mage. He grimaced and opened his eyes. Firelight flickered, casting unsteady shadows above. The smell of mildew and dampness invaded his nostrils. A sudden pain shot through his skull. He groaned.

Immediately, a hand touched his forehead. "You awake, mister?"

The touch of leathery fingers and the sound of a strangled voice startled Mage. He opened his eyes and stared into a shadowy face. He blinked once or twice. "Who—who are you?"

The man turned so the firelight reflected on his face. "It's me, mister. Joe. You remember? You gave me a blanket and a knife. You saved my life."

Mage squinted into the darkness. He grinned weakly. "I'm mighty glad to see you, Joe. Mighty glad." He paused and tried to penetrate the darkness with his eyes. "Where are we?"

Joe offered Mage a wooden bowl with steaming liquid in it. "Joe got good place. Nobody find you here."

Sitting up, Mage cupped the bowl in both hands and sipped the liquid. It was hot, not too tasty, but it warmed him as it trickled down his throat.

"I puts special herbs that takes away the hurt, mister. Drink it all down."

After he drained the bowl, Mage lay back. Moments later, he was sleeping.

Joe studied him a moment, then pulling aside the hide that served as a door, the old man slipped out into the forest.

Mage slept through the night. When he awakened next morning, he was hungry as a winter-starved wolf. He made short work of the broiled rabbit and herb tea Joe had put together.

The side of his head throbbed. He touched it and felt a knot the size of an egg covered with an oily salve.

Joe explained. "Special salve, Mister. Draws out de hurt and takes down de swelling. Whoever shoots at you, almost done what he wanted to do."

"Yeah. Reckon you're right." He looked around. "Where are we? Inside a tree?"

"Yes, sir. Big old oak. Must be three hunnerd years old. Had to chase out a few coons and snakes, but it be all right now."

Mage laughed, and his head began to spin. He put out a hand to steady himself. "I think I better lay back down."

"Yes, sir. You lays down. You finc here. Ain't nobody going to find you here. I guarantees that. You rest here."

Mage wanted to protest, to insist that he couldn't take time to rest, but before he could part his lips, he fell asleep.

Joe squatted by the fire, his chin resting on his arms that were wrapped around his knees.

Throughout the next twenty-four hours, Joe tended Mage tirelessly. To Mage, time blurred. He was vaguely aware of the hot broth and sweet water and the damp rag bathing his sweaty face.

When he awakened the third morning, his head was clear and the swelling had mostly subsided. The aroma of broiling meat made his mouth water.

Then he remembered Rachel and the children back at the Bar X. Abruptly, he started to rise, but a wave of dizziness caused him to slump back. He squeezed his eyes shut in an effort to slow the spinning in his skull.

"You got to be careful, mister. That there rifle ball mighta juggled something around in your head. Just rest a minute and eat a bite."

Clenching his teeth, Mage nodded briefly. "I got to get back to the Bar X."

Joe grunted and handed Mage a spit of broiled meat. "Here. Eat. Where de Bar X be?"

"Back northwest," Mage replied, slowly opening his eyes. The spinning had stopped. He grinned weakly at Joe and drew his tongue over his dry lips. "I could use some water."

Joe handed him a cupful, which he eagerly drained. "That was better than any drink of whiskey I ever had," he mumbled.

"Eat, mister. You feels better."

The broiled meat was tasty. When Mage reached for a second spit, he complimented the old man. "Right good. What is it?"

"Possum."

For a moment, Mage hesitated, then shrugged and kept eating. "I need a horse," he said between bites.

"I gots yours."

Mage looked at him in surprise.

"Gots him in the middle of a windfall a piece from here. Leastwise, I guesses it be yours. Found him in the woods after the one what shot you rode away."

With a chuckle, Mage shook his head slowly. "You are a surprise, Joe. One big surprise."

The leathery old man grinned, revealing several missing teeth.

Licking the last of the possum grease from his fingers, Mage fixed his eyes on Joe. With firm resolve in his voice, he said. "I got to go. I been here, what? Two days? Three days? I got to go."

Joe didn't argue. He heard the determination in Mage's voice. "I gets your horse."

After Joe disappeared, Mage slowly rose to his feet, using the interior of the tree trunk for support. He stood unsteadily for a few moments, but quickly, he regained his equilibrium and looked around the hollow tree trunk. His hat and gunbelt lay in a pile on one side.

Slowly, he squatted to retrieve his gear, half expecting the dizziness to return, but gratified when it did not. He strapped his gunbelt on and stepped outside. He placed his hat on one side of his head, avoiding the tender spot above his temple. There was a faint throbbing at the back of his eyeballs.

Overhead, through the canopy the sky was bright blue. The breeze soughed through the treetops, rattling the pine needles and hickory leaves softly.

Moments later, Joe returned with the pony. Mage grinned. "You saved me a long walk, Joe. I'm much obliged."

Joe stared up at him solemnly. "I owes you, mister. You saves my life."

Mage stuck out his hand. "You did the same for me, Joe. I reckon that makes us even."

The old man stared at the extended hand, then looked up into Mage's eyes in disbelief. Mage grinned. "Don't you want to shake?"

A broad grin lit Joe's face. He grabbed Mage's hand and shook it vigorously. "Yes, sir, yes, sir. I sure does want to shake your hand."

Mage tightened the cinch on his pony and climbed unsteadily into the saddle. He sat motionless for a moment, catching his breath. Finally, he looked down at the old man. "Joe, why don't you come with me? It's too dangerous out here. I know you got along so far, but sooner or later, your luck's going to run out." He pointed to the knife inside Joe's cloth belt. "That won't do you no good against Winchesters."

A deep frown creased Joe's forehead. He took a step back.

"I know how white people feel about you and your people. I can't stop that, but with me, you'll always have a friend that'll stick by you. Besides, I'm heading for California to join up with my brothers running a gambling hall. You can work for us out there, and from what I hear, there's all colors of folks there from all over the world."

Joe remained silent.

Mage leaned over and offered his hand. "Grab hold and swing behind me."

For several moments, Joe hesitated, then, "Waits for me. I gots to get my plunder." He disappeared inside the tree, reappearing moments later with the blanket Mage had given him. "I's ready."

With a click of his tongue, Mage headed due west. He wanted to swing by the Star B and warn them that someone was rustling their cattle.

The throbbing at the back of his eyes intensified.

Chapter Fourteen

Earlier, twenty miles to the southwest, Shank Hughes reined up beside Lutie Cole on the rim overlooking Black Draw. He removed his battered hat and dragged the back of his forearm across his sweaty brow. A cloud of dust lay just above the ground.

Below, over four hundred head of Star B stock milled about, grazing on the lush grass and drinking from the cool waters of the creek.

Cole cut his eyes toward Hughes and squirted a stream of brown tobacco juice on the sand. "They look mighty good down there."

With a snort, Hughes tugged his hat back on his head. "They'll look a heap better when we got the rest of them down there." He waved the other riders over.

Slim Bachelor was down below stringing the last of the

rope corral to keep the stock in. He waved to Hughes. "Another minute." Finally, he snugged down the last knot and swung into the saddle.

With his cohorts gathered around, Hughes quickly gave the orders. "Slim, you and Lutie get back to your spreads. Don't forget to meet the noon rider." He turned to Mustang Bill Lewis and Cooter Perl. "You two make sure the animals can't get out of the draw, then head over to the Circle L. Start rounding up old man Madeley's stock on the south range. I want us to start moving them this afternoon. We've already taken too long."

Perl gave Lewis a sidelong glance. Lewis nodded. "Don't worry none, Shank. We'll be there."

His eyes went cold. "You best. I want them beeves here tomorrow if we got to push 'em all night."

Cole whined. "What're you pushing so hard for, Shank? Why, them folks in town are getting sicker and sicker. Ain't none of them be able to fork a horse for the next two weeks according to what the mayor told me yesterday."

Hughes' eyes turned to ice. "You want what Bob Dawkins got?"

Cole gulped. He shook his head. "No, Shank."

"Then you do what I say. We don't get those beeves here tomorrow, I reckon I'll just up and kill someone. You hear?"

The old man nodded vigorously although he figured Hughes was joshing, maybe. "You bet, Shank. Don't you worry none. We'll have 'em here."

Mage was weaker than he thought. He pulled into the shade of a motte of oak to catch his breath before he spotted the Star B. As he anticipated, it was deserted. Cautiously, he circled the main house and the empty outbuildings. A few head of cattle milled about. Several ponies nickered from the corral.

For a moment, he considered taking a horse for Joe and leaving a note with payment for the animal. But, given the circumstances, he figured the fewer who knew he was still alive, the better.

"Reckon ain't nobody here, mister."

Staring at the ponies, Mage replied. "Looks that way, Joe." Though he had no hard proof, Mage would have bet every cent he had that the missing ranch hands were the rustlers.

He glanced at the sun, then dropped his gaze on the road to town. From what he had been told, the Star B was about five or six miles from town. The sheriff had set up a meeting everyday at noon on the road into town. It wasn't quite noon. If they hurried, they might find the rider from town as well as one of the ranch hands. Maybe they could tell him what was going on.

The sorrel could not stand up to carrying double at a gallop. Within a few hundred yards, the gelding stumbled, then caught itself.

Muttering a curse, Mage reined the laboring animal into a slow trot. He squinted his eyes against the sunlight. His head throbbed painfully. The sun baked down, reflecting its heat off the hardpan beneath the pony's feet.

Dropping the reins over the saddle horn, Mage reached for his canteen. He removed his hat and poured water over his head, then gulped a couple swallows. He handed it back to Joe who took a couple sips.

Ahead, a dark figure appeared in the road. Moments later, another rider appeared, this one to Mage's left, coming over a rise about half a mile distant.

All three spotted each other at the same time.

They continued riding.

Ten minutes later, they reined up, ten yards apart. Mage felt Joe press up against his back, but he dismissed it figuring the old man was frightened of the two white men.

Mage grinned at first when he saw C.A. Webb, but the grin turned to a frown when he got a better look at the storeowner. The other rider, a wrangler, was a stranger.

A spasm of coughing seized the storeowner. Instinctively, Mage started to his side, but Webb held up his hand. "No, schoolteacher. I'm contagious. I got the cholera on me, Doc says. Stay back."

Shank Hughes recognized the horse Mage rode. It was the one that had raced past him in the forest a few days earlier. And he had heard of the schoolteacher, but he had never met him. His eyes narrowed, wondering where the teacher had been the last two or three days. "What about the town? Anything changed since yesterday?" He asked the question of Webb, but his eyes kept straying back to Mage and the old man behind the saddle.

Joe pressed tighter against Mage's back.

"About the same. No one died. We've had eight so far, but looks like we might be starting to hold our own."

Hughes spoke up. "Anything you need us to do?"

Weakly, Webb replied. "Just keep looking after things, Shank. I reckon everything is okay."

Hughes cut his eyes toward Mage. "Yep. Tell them in town that everything's running smooth out here."

Mage turned to Hughes. "You one of the Star B riders?"

The rustler's eyes narrowed. "Reckon I am. I don't know you though, stranger."

"I'm the schoolteacher. What about you?"

"Shank Hughes. I ride for Mr. Brewster. Him and his missus was in town with our other riders when the sickness come in. I been looking after things."

Webb interrupted. "I thought Bob Dawkins was riding out here too."

"Huh? Oh, yeah. Old Bob. He's back at the ranch house. I been checking stock back south." As he spoke, his hand drifted down to the butt of his six-shooter.

Something was wrong. Mage felt that tingling at the base of his skull. No one was around the ranch when they were there less than an hour earlier. "Having any trouble with the cattle?"

Fire flashed in Hughes' black eyes. His thick frame straightened. "Trouble? Why should I?"

Mage shrugged and plastered an amiable grin on his face. "Just figured. Only the two of you with all them cows. Keep a hombre hustling."

Hughes relaxed. "Naw. We ain't had no trouble. Them cows is just standing about, eating and drinking, fat and sassy."

"You're lucky. Back up at the Bar X, we had to move cows to fresh water." It was a lie, and he waited anxiously for Hughes' response.

"Not us. C.A. knows all the water we got at Cherokee Wells. We ain't got to take them cows nowhere." He nodded to Joe. "What you doing with him?"

For the first time, Webb noticed Joe. He frowned at Mage, who replied, "Found him back northeast apiece. Down on his luck, so I figured to give him a hand."

Arching an eyebrow, Hughes replied, "Watch out that he don't steal everything you got."

Mage felt Joe trembling against his back. He ignored Hughes' warning. "C.A., you best get back to town. Get some rest." He touched his fingers to the brim of his hat and nodded to Hughes. "Good luck." Wheeling about, Mage cut north across the prairie, grateful that Webb was still with Hughes.

As they topped the first rise and dropped out of sight, Joe eased his grip on Mage. "He was the one, mister. He was the one what shot you with that rifle gun."

Cold fear chilled Mage's blood when he and Joe rode up to the Bar X and witnessed the devastation brought about by the marauding Comanche. The only structures remaining were the main house and the corrals, which had been patched with rawhide, and in which milled a few horses. Moments later, the doors flew open and the children along with Rachel and Laura rushed out, shouting and laughing.

Later, around the kitchen table and with a pot of steaming black coffee, Rachel related their battle with the Comanche. Mage clenched his jaw. "Seen any around since then?"

She shook her head. "I haven't, but Robert there says he saw sign."

Robert nodded. "Yes, sir. About a quarter-mile north, over the rise. I run across fresh signs. Best I could guess, four, maybe five Indian ponies. The same number that rode out of here after burning the barn and chuckhouse."

Rachel looked at the swelling above Mage's temple. "What about you? Where have you been?"

He chuckled. "Seems like trouble dogs all of us." He touched the side of his head. "I got shot. By a man rustling Star B cattle."

The Brewster boys stiffened. "What? Why, we got to stop them," William blurted out.

Mage continued. "Take it easy. I know who they are— one, maybe two. We'll take care of them."

Rachel spoke up. "You say one of them shot you?"

"Yep, and I might have been a goner if Joe hadn't found me." Briefly, he related the events since he had ridden out.

When they learned how Joe had saved Mage, they couldn't do enough for the old man. Laura dug out a set of her son's fresh clothes, brogans and all.

The new set of clothes hung from Joe's thin frame, but the old man grinned like a sassy little raccoon. It was the first time in years he had donned any type of clothing that wasn't ragged and holey.

"We ain't see no sign of rustlers up around here around the Bar X, Mr. Casebolt," William said.

"That's because you're here. I'm guessing they're working the other spreads. Most of the wranglers are in town. Best I understand, there's only a couple at each ranch. I figure they're our rustlers. Moving a few thousand head down to Houston or over to a trail drive would put a heap of gold in a jasper's pocket. Mighty big temptation."

William Brewster leaned forward. "So what are we going to do? We can't let nobody steal all the cattle."

Mage glanced at Rachel. He saw the apprehension in her eyes. Forcing a grin, he said. "We won't, but first, we got to be sure that's what those old boys are up to. I figure it is. The one named Shank claims they weren't moving cattle, but I saw the herd moving south. And Joe here says it was Shank who gave me this." He touched his finger to the raw gouge above his temple. "And I spotted a Circle L rider pushing Star B stock. Still, we got to be sure."

Robert exclaimed. "I can't believe Shank is part of this. He's been with us four, five years."

"I can," William growled. "I never cared for him no way."

"Regardless," Mage repeated, "we've got to be sure."

"Sounds like it's sure enough," William snapped. "What about him shooting at you?"

"He could of thought I was a rustler."

"What about moving the cattle?"

Mage grimaced. "I can't argue that, but I still want to be certain."

Rachel arched an eyebrow. "And how do you plan on doing that?"

He studied her a moment. "I'm not really sure." He looked at William and Robert. "If you wanted to hide some cows for a few days, where would you put them? Anyplace like that around Valley Springs, say ten, twelve miles?"

The boys considered the question. Robert glanced at William sheepishly, then said. "There's a place southwest. A creek with steep banks. Black Draw. A jasper can hide a heap of cows in Black Draw."

William frowned at his brother. "How do you know? Turk warned us never to go down there. How do you know?"

Robert shrugged. "I just do."

"When did you go down there?"

"None of your business."

A slow light of understanding lit William's eyes. "Is that where you and Molly Simmons disappeared last year during the Easter egg hunt at the Circle L?"

"I told you it's none of your business."

"Just you wait 'til I tell Pa."

Mage grinned at Rachel, then broke up the argument. "That's enough, boys. We got more to worry about than an Easter egg hunt. Now, Robert, there is room in that draw to hold cows?"

"Yes sir. It's real long and wide with steep bluffs. All you have to do is fence it off at either end. There's plenty of graze and water so the cows won't get restless."

Rachel spoke up. "What are you going to do, Mage?"

A sudden weariness flooded over him. "First, I want a nap. Then tonight, me and Robert are going to take a ride."

"Hold on," William interrupted. "If Robert's going, I'm going too."

Mage shook his head. "No, boy. You stay here in case the Comanche decides to pay a visit. Robert knows where Black Draw is. That's why he's going. If it was the other way round, you'd go. Understand? I need a man to stay here."

Grimacing, William nodded. "Yeah, I reckon I see what you mean, but I don't like it."

Turning back to Robert, Mage said. "How far is the draw?"

"Twenty-five miles, give or take a few."

Mage whistled "That's six hours easy riding, maybe three if we pushed the horses, but that would probably kill them. If we leave about sundown, we should be back north of Valley Springs before sunrise."

"I go too, mister."

"No, Joe. You stay here."

The old man glanced around nervously.

Mage calmed him. "You're with friends here, Joe."

"He's right, Joe," Laura said. "You're family now."

"What about horses?" Mage hooked his thumb toward the corrals. "Them out there good for an all-night run?"

William nodded. "All night and all day."

"Good. Get 'em ready. We're pulling out at sundown."

Chapter Fifteen

William knew his horseflesh.

They threw their saddles on two long-legged, deep-chested geldings that looked to have staying power. Around ten or eleven, they spotted dim lights a mile or so to the east. "Valley Springs," Robert said.

The night was clear. Mage glanced west, in the direction of the Triple X, but no lights appeared in the darkness.

Despite the urgency and possible danger of their mission, Mage was awed by the country through which he rode. He had never seen anything so vast, or so silent.

Later, Robert pulled up. In a whisper, he said, "If I got my direction straight, Black Draw is over that next rise." They sat motionless in their saddles, ears tuned to the night around them.

"I don't hear nothing."

"I told you, Mr. Casebolt. Black Draw's got plenty grass and water. I reckon you could keep a heap of cows fat and satisfied down there."

"I'll take a look," Mage said, dismounting and handing the reins to Robert. "You stay here."

Dropping into a crouch, he made his way to the crest of the rise and dropped to his belly. A quarter of a mile distant, he made out a broad black hole in the ground that seemed to stretch to the horizon. To his right, the starlight glimmered faintly on a winding ribbon of water that disappeared into the gaping fissure.

Black Draw!

He strained his ears for any sound of cattle. He heard nothing. He had to be sure cattle were in the draw. Slowly, he rose into a crouch and glided down the rise to the edge of the draw.

The shadows were thick down in the draw, but as his eyes grew accustomed to the darkness, he could make out several beeves sleeping contentedly.

He suppressed the surge of excitement racing through his blood. A few sleeping cows didn't translate into a band of rustlers, but a temporary fence across the mouth of the draw certainly would.

Easing along the rim, Mage made his way to the west opening of the draw and followed the creek down into its depths. The opening was a bottleneck, and where the neck broadened, Mage discovered ropes strung from one side to the other, held in place by fresh cut posts sunk into the ground. The vertical walls on either side rose at least ten, twelve feet.

Glancing at the rim of the draw above, Mage whipped out his knife and slashed the ropes. If nothing else, the rustlers would have to spend extra time rounding up the cows that strayed through the bottleneck.

When he finished, he sheathed his knife and peered through the darkness toward Valley Springs.

To the east, the rising sun struggled to penetrate the thick clouds rolling in from the southeast. A brisk breeze rushed headlong across the prairie, leaving sweeping footsteps in the tall grass. Mage and Robert pulled up on the outskirts of Valley Springs. "This is far enough," Mage said. The nearest structure was the schoolhouse, some fifty yards distant.

The young boy frowned at Mage. "You mean because of the sickness?"

Mage nodded. "I don't know much about how contagious cholera is, son. For all I know, we might be able to brush shoulders without catching it. But I don't particularly favor taking that kind of chance."

"Me neither."

At that moment, a face appeared in one of the schoolhouse windows, then quickly vanished. Moments later, Doc Shelby appeared from around the corner of the building. He stopped some twenty yards from them. "What are you doing here? We're still contagious." A gust of wind tousled his thin gray hair.

"You're the one I wanted to see, Doc. How close can we get? I got some serious news that don't need to be spread unless it's absolutely necessary."

Doc Shelby mulled the question. "Reckon we can come a little closer. You stay there. I'll come to you."

Mage lowered his voice. "We got problems, Doc. Bad problems. Rustlers are hitting the Star B and Circle L. I figure they'll hit the Triple X too. They're holding the cattle in Black Draw."

Doc Shelby's haggard face became even more gaunt. His shoulders sagged. "Who's doing it?"

"I don't know all of them, but Shank Hughes is one. Lutie Cole is another."

"Hughes?" He shot a surprised look at Robert. "Why he's your daddy's foreman."

Mage shrugged. "I don't know about that, but he's one of them. He's the one that put this knot on my head. You got anyone well enough to fork a horse?"

Wearily, the old physician shook his head. "Every one of them is sicker than a trailhand after a two-day drink. They couldn't last ten minutes in the saddle. We lost two more last night."

"You reckon we ought to tell them about the rustlers?"

Doc Shelby considered Mage's question. "I suppose they deserve to know, but if I was to tell 'em, they'd lose all sense and try to ride out. They'd all be dead in less than an hour. I can barely keep enough liquid in them now." He looked up at Robert. "How you doing, boy?"

Robert grinned crookedly and ducked his head into the wind. "Fine, Doc, except for the Comanche."

Doc Shelby looked around at Mage in alarm. The teacher nodded. "That's the other problem, Doc. They hit a few days ago and skedaddled. Seen some signs since, but not a hair on their head. We got plenty guns and ammunition, and the Barton house is like a fort."

"I know," Doc Shelby replied. "I remember when John built the place." He hesitated. "You best head back. I'd rest easier knowing you was back there with them kids." He chewed on his bottom lip. "I don't think I'm going to say nothing about the Comanche. It isn't as if their raids are anything new. Just you take care of the kids."

"What about the rustlers, Doc?"

The old man shrugged. "We can raise more cows. Just take care of the kids."

* * *

Shank Hughes tugged his hat down tight against the wind and glared at Cooter Perl who had just brought news that three hundred head of cattle had wandered out of the draw after someone cut the ropes holding the stock in. "You didn't see no one?"

Cooter shook his head. "Found no sign neither. Them cows had tromped out any tracks. Good thing Mustang Bill rode up there. Otherwise, I reckon the whole shebang would have wandered away. He's rounding them up now."

Hughes cursed. He glanced northward to the road where he was supposed to meet the daily messenger from Valley Springs. Another day wasted. Worse than that, someone was on to them.

"Who do you reckon coulda done it?" Perl asked.

Stroking his wiry, black beard, Shank grunted. "Only jasper not in town is that schoolteacher."

Perl widened his eyes in surprise. "The schoolteacher? You think he's got the sand to do something like that?"

Hughes' eyes narrowed. His jaw grew hard. "You got any suggestions who else coulda done it?"

"But, what could he have done it for?"

"I got no idea," Hughes replied, lifting his gaze in the direction of the Bar X. "But I got me an itch that says he done it, and when I got an itch, I scratch it."

"What you got in mind, Shank?"

"Never you worry about it. I'll take care of that jasper. Meantime, you get back and help Mustang Bill get them cows back in the draw. I want to move the Triple X stock down tomorrow night."

Perl squinted at the thick clouds rushing past. "Gonna be darker'n the inside of a cow tonight if them clouds hang around."

"Just do what I said, you hear?"

"I hear." Perl gave a quick nod. "I hear."

* * *

Doc Shelby slumped down in an upholstered wingback chair in the lobby of the Excelsior. He was torn between the Hippocratic oath he had taken to do no harm, and the morality of keeping a secret of the rustling at Star B and Circle L. If he revealed Mage's accusations, every manjack in town would go boiling across the prairie, and probably drop dead within three miles.

No. Best to say nothing. Let the noon messengers keep going out. At least, the rustlers won't figure they've been discovered. He lifted his eyes to the heavens. "Dear Lord, why couldn't you have made me just a tad smarter?"

Back to the southeast, the clouds darkened. Thunder rumbled across the prairie.

Mage leaned back in his chair and studied the others seated around the kitchen table—Joe, Rachel, Laura, and the Brewster brothers. The younger children were playing Jack Straws in front of the fireplace in the main room.

"I don't cotton to the idea of letting the rustlers have the stock, but I understand Doc Shelby's point," Mage said. "Our best bet is to sit here, protect the kids from the Comanche. We got sufficient cartridges. Long as we stay inside, no one can touch us."

William nodded. "Yeah. The only way anyone could get us out of here is blow the place up."

They all grinned, but they had no idea that William had accurately predicted the future.

Night settled over the Bar X, bringing with it a darkness made even darker by the thick layer of clouds rolling past. Thunder boomed, and occasional flashes of lightning slashed across the heavens, casting the countryside in eerie white relief.

After the fire had burned down in the hearth, Mage felt

a hand on his shoulder. "Mr. Casebolt." It was William who had the midnight watch. "Wake up."

Mage sat up. "What?"

"I don't know for sure. Something's stirring up the horses."

Quickly padding across the floor, Mage peered through a gun port. The milling horses were darker shadows against the darkness of the night.

"What do you think? Comanche?"

Mage flinched as the sharp crash of lightning rattled the wooden shutters. The hair on the back of his neck bristled as a second flash of lightning froze a shadow outside the corral. The lightning flashed again, and the shadow had vanished. Mage blinked and strained to peer into the night. "I don't know, boy. Wake everybody up. Get the kids in the cellar."

Another streak of lightning revealed only the milling horses. Had he indeed seen a man? Or was it just a trick of shadows cast by bolts of lightning? Mage squinted into the darkness, searching around the dark hulk of the barn and chuckhouse, but nothing moved. He studied the wagon beside the corral. Nothing there. Behind him came the sounds of small feet scurrying down into the cellar.

He sensed Joe at his side. "You see anything?"

"No, mister. The kids are all in the cellar."

Without warning, a blinding light and thundering roar ripped through the darkness as the back room in which the children had been sleeping exploded. The shock wave knocked Mage backward into the wall, and the surge of heat seemed to singe the hair on his arms and face. The sharp odor of black powder told him instantly that the explosion was manmade.

He shouted. "The windows. Get to the windows, boys."

Lightning crashed once again. Mage glimpsed a dark figure on a horse, and then the night swallowed the apparition.

The wall separating the living area from the bedroom blazed. Mage grabbed a blanket and beat at the flames. "William, Robert! Stay at the windows."

Another explosion of thunder and crack of lightning. Gusts of wind howled through the fractured roof and shattered walls of the house, feeding fresh oxygen to the flames wildly leaping thirty feet into the dark sky.

Rachel brushed past him and hurled a bucket of water on the flames. Joe took her place. In the kitchen, Laura frantically pumped water into bucket after bucket.

"What do you see?" Mage shouted to the boys.

"Nothing. No Comanche. Nothing."

"Me neither," Robert called out over the booming thunder.

By now, the flames reached the wood shake roof. Mage grimaced and continued to flail at the flames with the blanket. "We can't stay here."

Without warning, a deluge of rain struck, a wall so thick and heavy that within minutes, the blazing fire was extinguished.

Mage herded the children into one corner of the kitchen. He put the boys at the back door and the window while he stood at the door to the living area, Winchester in hand.

The driving rain settled into a steady patter, drenching the house. Outside, nothing moved. The only sounds other than the rain were the occasional nickers from the horses in the corral. "You boys spot anything?"

"No, sir."

Laura spoke up. "You think we'd be safe to put on some coffee, Mage?"

"Not yet. Let me take a look around. William, you watch this door while I'm gone."

He glanced into the darkness of the kitchen behind him. He couldn't see Rachel's face, but he had the feeling she was watching him.

"Joe, I need your help." Mage crept across the rain-soaked living area to the gaping hole in the wall. He pressed up against the shattered logs. He could smell the odor of wet ashes as he peered around the jagged ends of the logs into the night.

Moments later, he slipped outside with Joe at his side, a .44 ball and cap pistol in the old man's hand. The lightning had passed over, heading northwest. The steady rain continued.

Dropping into a crouch, he eased toward the corral, pausing to peer into the burned out hulk of the barn, and inspecting the covered wagon where they had stored their saddles and tack since the Comanche burned the barn.

Mage looked around, the rain pattering against his face. "It looks clear to me."

Joe agreed. "There ain't nobody out here. Just us."

Squinting his eyes against the gusting rain, Mage searched the darkness surrounding them. "I hope you're right, Joe. I truly do."

Chapter Sixteen

The rain slackened into a steady drizzle, and the new morning dawned drab and gray. In the corral, the horses stood with their heads down, the water running off their necks and manes in rivulets.

"You gots any idea who did this, mister?" Joe's voice was a whisper in the drizzle.

Mage's voice was cold with fury. "I know who did it."

Joe remained silent a moment. "The same one what shot you?"

"Yeah."

With the rain came a chill, but the roaring fire in the woodstove quickly drove the dampness away. The rich aroma of fresh coffee filled the kitchen.

Mage's primary concern was the safety of the children.

"I figure the Comanche'll come back now. Even if the rustlers leave us alone, we couldn't stand off a war party here."

Laura shook her head. "You right certain Shank Hughes is behind all this?"

"Yes, ma'am." Mage nodded. "Joe here saw Shank try to gun me down. I saw him and a few others moving Star B stock south from Cherokee Wells. It was just after I spotted them that I got shot."

"But how'd he figure you was up here? At our place?"

Mage sipped his coffee. "Everybody in town knew we brought the kids up here. It wasn't a secret."

Rachel chewed on her bottom lip. "We've got to decide what to do. We can't go into town."

William spoke up. "What about our place? There's plenty room."

"We could, but Shank and his boys know of your place. If we disappear from here, they'll search every one of your folks' places. What we need is someplace they don't know about."

"I knows a place."

Everyone fell silent and stared at Joe. His damp clothes hung from his thin frame. "Back in de woods, I found me a cave. It be on the side of a big hill that don't look like no hill."

Mage leaned forward. "Near where you found me?"

He shook his head. "No, mister. It be back north a piece."

Mage grinned at Rachel. Maybe this was what he was looking for. "How big is it?" He gestured to the children. "We got a bunch here."

Joe raised his arms and made a large circle of them. "More than enough. Room for the wagon and animals too."

A wave of excitement washed over Mage. Here was the chance to keep the kids safe plus afford him the time to figure out how to foil the rustlers' plans. But, he cautioned himself, he would not go after the rustlers unless the children were absolutely safe.

He looked at Rachel. He saw the approval in her eyes. "You think you'll have any trouble finding the place, Joe?"

"No, Sir. Like cutting open a watermelon."

"How far?"

"We be there by dark if we leave now." He paused. "But, there's something bad there too, mister."

"Bad? What?"

"A heap of small tunnels run out from the big cave. They's got holes that go down deep into the belly of the earth."

Rachel gasped.

"But the cave is safe? I mean, as long as we don't go back into the tunnels."

Joe nodded. "That's right. They safe."

Mage looked at the two women. "Well, ladies. I reckon we know what we got to do."

Forcing a smile, Laura nodded. "Reckon we do."

Outside, the drizzle continued. They were in for a wet trip, Mage told himself.

While Mage and Joe hooked up the team, the others filled the covered wagon with supplies, foodstuffs, blankets, rifles, ammunition, and a miscellany of other items.

William drove the wagon with the ladies and children inside. The pucker holes were snugged down tight to keep out the drizzle. Robert brought up the rear, leading the remaining horses. Mage and Joe took the lead.

The prairie absorbed the rain, letting the life-giving water drain quickly down to the roots thirsting for a drink. The iron wheels cut into the wet soil, leaving a clear trail for anyone to follow.

Mage crossed his fingers, hoping for the drizzle to continue. The consistency of the wet sand produced sharp tracks that melted quickly in the rain. Enough rain, and the sand would flow into the tracks, removing all sign of their passage except for the most practiced eye.

Not long before sunset, they reached the forest. Dismounting, Joe snapped a lead rope on the O-ring of the bridle of the near lead horse on the team. "We walk," he said, looking up at Mage. "Animals don't spook easy like that."

Without hesitating, Joe unerringly led them on a winding course through the trees deep into the loblolly pines. Overhead, gray clouds scudded over the treetops, but night was fast approaching.

Mage looked at the slight figure leading the wagon. "How much farther?"

"Not long."

Mage looked around, concerned with the encroaching darkness. "It'll be pitch black in a few minutes."

"I know the place, mister. I gets us there."

Somehow, the old man's words eased Mage's concern. He couldn't explain why, but he believed Joe. Over his shoulder, he called softly back to the wagon. "Not long now."

Joe continued his steady pace, twisting through the forest even after dark shadows filled the woods. Mage lost sense of direction.

Finally, Joe halted. He handed Mage the lead rope. "You wait." Before Mage could reply, the old man vanished into the darkness. Off in the darkness came the sounds of snapping branches. Moments later, a pale yellow glow flickered off in the night.

The light of the torch grew brighter. Joe called out as he pushed through a tangle of vines. "This be the place I tell you about." He held the torch over his head, the glow of which revealed the entrance to the cave, which towered several feet above the wagon.

With Mage on one side of the entrance and the two Swink boys on the other side holding the vines back, Joe led the wagon into the cave. When the Brewster brothers and the horses had passed, Mage and the boys dropped the vines back in place and followed the wagon around a bend in the cave.

Around the bend, the cave opened into a great room that gave mute evidence of having been used over the centuries by transient Indians.

Mage looked around in awe. "Any other way in?"

"I don't find none, mister," Joe replied, shaking his head, holding the torch higher. The flames flickered, dancing first in one direction and then the other.

Mage took note then, with a grin, he looked up at Rachel. "This is what I was looking for."

She shivered and cast a hurried glance around the cave. "Caves are spooky. I get goosebumps."

Mage laughed and helped her down. "A warm fire and a good meal, you'll feel a heap better."

As the boys put together a small fire from dry wood they found strewn about the cave, Mage studied their refuge. From the way the flames of the torch danced about, there had to be other entrances. He couldn't imagine any tribe of Indians putting themselves in a spot from which they could not retreat.

He scanned the sandy floor, looking for tracks, sign of what kind of humans or animals had been living in the cave. He found the usual possum and raccoon sign, a pad print of either a large coyote or small wolf, centipede tracks, but no sign of the one creature of which he was most concerned other than man, the black bear.

Naturally, stories of bloodthirsty creatures, especially the bear, followed all immigrants. Most of the stories were simply that, stories—stories created by natives to frighten new-comers. But in his entire journey from New Orleans, all of which had been along rural tracks, he had only seen one black bear, and when the creature spotted him, it promptly vanished into the forest.

Still, a jasper couldn't afford to take chances. Before he left to take care of the rustlers, he would lay out a plan that would keep the children safe just in case one should wander past.

That night, Mage rolled up in a blanket near the entrance to the cave. Several times, he jerked awake, but the night passed uneventfully.

Next morning, he arose and stood at the mouth of the cave. The rain had ceased, but water still dripped from the vines. He stepped outside the cave and caught his breath.

Far to the east, the sun painted the distant clouds a bright red. He had wondered what Joe had meant about a big hill, and now he saw. Stretching away below him was a great bowl of a valley, thick with stands of oak and hickory and loblolly pine and sloping down from the cave in a gradual descent some two, maybe three hundred feet and spreading almost a mile to the north and south and to the horizon back to the east.

Ten, perhaps even twenty savannahs of lush grass dotted the valley, and Mage made out dark objects in the middle of the islands of grass. Feeding deer, he guessed.

He shook his head. He had never seen a more glorious sight. If a jasper were looking to settle and raise a family, he couldn't find a better spot.

Tearing his eyes away from the valley, he studied the forest around him. Moving silently, he eased back along the tracks they had made the night before, noting that Joe had not led them along a trail or trace, but through the middle of the unmarked forest.

A mile or so from the cave, he reached the tree line,

from inside of which he peered out across the prairie. In the distance, half a dozen deer paused on the crest of a hill looking back at him, their pricked ears looking like white flags. He remained still. Moments later, they dropped their heads and went back to grazing, all except for a large doe that continued watching.

Mage grinned, but remained frozen in place. No telling who else might be observing the deer. More than once, Mage and old Doc Bender had taken advantage of the behavior of their animals to avoid ambushes and bushwhackers. The way a pony perked his ears, or shied, or grew nervous spoke volumes. A jasper just needed to pay attention.

Mage made his way back to the cave where he laid out his plans for the next day or so. "Joe, you and William stay here. I'll take Robert with me." He went on to explain how the two of them would stay within the tree line and skirt the prairie around to Black Draw. "If they've pushed the cows out, we can find the trail easy enough."

Rachel looked up from the fire where she was frying bacon. "What if they haven't?"

"Well, then, maybe we can figure out some way to slow them down."

William spoke up. "Mr. Casebolt. Instead of me just sitting here, why can't I meet the messenger from town and tell them what's going on? Maybe Sheriff Swink can help."

Mage shook his head briefly. "Sure like to, son, but it's too dangerous. Shank or one of his boys might grab you. No, you stay here with Joe to look after things. The Doc said the sheriff couldn't sit on a horse for fifteen minutes. No sense in upsetting a jasper about something he can't do nothing about."

The young man fell silent. Seemed like there was more he could do than just babysit a bunch of children.

Rachel fixed Mage with a look of defiance in her eyes.

"Personally, I don't think you need to be out gallivanting around. If you're going to take Doc Shelby's advice, then stay here. We all stay here until it's safe."

He studied her several moments. "It's bad enough those old boys are rustling the cows. But it's doubly bad that they're doing it to folks too sick to try to stop 'em. That's like kicking a jasper when he's down. There's nothing right about that. Not at all. Somebody has to try to stop them."

She glared at him. Her voice trembled with frustration. "And you're going to try."

A crooked grin played over his lips. "Yes, ma'am. I most certainly am."

Sarcasm dripped from her words. "And suppose you tell us just how you're going to stop them."

He stared back at her, his ears burning. He had no idea what he was going to do, only that he had to make the effort. "I don't reckon I'll know until I see what we're up against."

She shook her head and twisted her lips into a wry grin. "You ever stop to think it might be too late by then?"

"Yes, ma'am, I have."

"So?"

"So, if I see it's too late, then Robert and me'll turn around and ride back here."

And he knew that's what they would finally do. Ride back, for there was no way he could stop Shank Hughes and the rustlers. Not with the children. But stubbornly, he rode out, hoping for a miracle.

Chapter Seventeen

Over eight hundred head of cattle milled about in Black Draw. By now, the lush bluestem and grama had been eaten to the ground, and banks of the creek had been churned into mud.

Shank Hughes sat on his deep-chested black. The animal's wide set eyes rolled wildly and his broad nostrils flared. Hughes jerked the bit cruelly in the black's mouth. The burly cowpoke cursed the animal. "I'll tear that devil head off if you don't stop yanking on the bit."

Cooter Perl pulled up beside Hughes and looked over the backs of the stirring cows. "All we need now is the Triple X stock. Slim has moved them south of the ranch. Him and me ought to have the herd within five or six miles by noon."

Hughes lifted one side of his lips in a sneer. "About time. We can push 'em in here tonight and move out in the morning. A week or so, we'll have 'em down to Houston."

Perl cleared his throat. "What about them kids and the schoolteacher?"

"No telling where they be." Hughes narrowed his black eyes and stared back to the north. "Rain washed out the signs. For all I know, they might have gone to town and took their chances with the sickness." He reined his horse around. The big animal pulled on the bit and snorted. "Forget about them. It's time for me to get back to the east road."

William Brewster looked on as the girls played Hunt the Slipper in the light of the fire, and Rachel and Laura attempted to keep the boys from wandering back into the dark tunnels networking out from the large room. Joe had gone outside not long after Mage and Robert rode out.

Chafing at the fact he had to play nursemaid while rustlers were stealing his pa's cows, William decided he would do what he could to stop them despite the promises he had made the teacher.

The teacher.

In a burst of righteous indignation, William reminded himself that Casebolt wasn't no teacher. He was a two-bit gambler. That's what his pa said. And Casebolt was so dumb that the mayor and others had suckered him into taking over the school job until the new schoolmarm arrived.

He didn't owe Casebolt nothing.

Quickly, he saddled one of their ponies and slid a Winchester in the boot. Rachel spotted him as he rode out. "William! William!" But he ignored her.

By the time Joe spotted the young man, William was already a hundred yards deep in the forest.

Mid-morning, Mage and Robert reined up inside the tree line. On the horizon, a speck moved north. It was a rider, but the distance was too great to make out any details.

"Who do you reckon that is, Mr. Casebolt?"

"Don't know, son, but from the way he's moving, he's no drifter, so I'm guessing it's one of the rustlers." He wheeled his pony around and touched his heels to the animal's flanks. "Let's us make some time, boy. I got me a feeling that no one is watching the herd at Black Draw right now."

"What do you plan on doing, Mr. Casebolt? You think we can stop them from taking the herd?"

Mage glanced at the boy. He had no idea. He tried to make himself believe they would stumble onto a solution, but deep down, he knew their task was hopeless. Still, he stubbornly clung to an outside hope. "I'm not sure, Robert. Let's see when we get there."

The sun was directly overhead when Mage and Robert spotted the draw. They pulled up inside the trees and studied the open mile of short grass prairie between them and the creek.

"I don't see nobody around, Mr. Casebolt."

"Just take it easy. We got time." Mage guessed that three of the rustlers were at their daily meeting with the messengers from town. The other two were probably pushing Triple X stock toward the draw.

After ten minutes of careful scrutiny of the rolling countryside, Mage urged his pony from the forest. Robert followed on his heels. They kicked their cowhorses into a lope, quickly eating up the mile between them and the draw.

Robert whistled when they pulled up on the rim of the

draw. "Jeepers, Mr. Casebolt. There must be a thousand head or so down there."

Mage ran his gaze along the draw, surprised himself at the number of milling beeves filling the half-mile long draw. "I don't know how many's down there, boy, but there's a heap of them."

"What are we going to do?" The young man was looking around anxiously. "I don't see no one. We'd better get a move on at whatever we got to do."

An unbidden grin played over Mage's lips. "Reckon you're right, boy. I'm getting kinda antsy too. You got a knife?"

"Yes, sir. A Barlow."

"We can't stop them. Not you and me, but we can slow them down some until maybe we can think of something. You jump down there and cut the ropes keeping them in. Then hightail it back to the tree line. I'll do the same down at the other end."

With a click of his tongue, Mage headed his pony along the rim. He glanced over his shoulder to see the young man disappear down into the draw. By the time he reached the end of the draw, Robert was climbing back on his pony. He waved to Mage who gestured to the forest.

Quickly, Mage dismounted, stomped through the mud, sliced the ropes, clambered back up and gathered two or three bunches of dried grass.

Touching a match to the grass torches, he tossed them among the milling cattle, then swung into his saddle and raced back to the timber.

Hidden by the shadows of the forest, Mage and Robert grinned in satisfaction as cattle boiled out of either end of the draw. Within minutes, long-legged beeves began spreading across the prairie.

"Well, I reckon they be spending some time rounding up that bunch."

Robert looked up at Mage. "But what are we going to do then?"

A wave of frustration washed over Mage. He drew a deep breath and released it slowly. He had refused to face the inevitable, but the pure, unvarnished truth was there was nothing they could do to stop the rustlers. "The only thing I can see is that we can slow them down, but that won't stop them."

"Why don't we surprise them. Maybe we can catch them asleep or something."

Mage chuckled. "No, son. Your ma and pa left you to me. Now, I figure I've probably stretched it some bringing you with me out here, but there ain't no way on this earth you younkers are going to get mixed up in something that'll get you hurt, or worse."

Mage wheeled his pony around. "I reckon we got a couple hours before it gets exciting around here. Best we get back to the others."

During the ride back to the cave, Mage decided that the only way he and Joe just might have a chance of stopping the herd is if they struck from ambush. He hesitated. Not Joe. The old man couldn't move fast enough.

He'd have to do it himself. If he hit hard and sudden, then disappeared. Maybe he could whittle them down one at a time. It would be chancy, but it was better than sitting on his hands and just watching the rustlers make off with the herd.

Back to the west, the sun dropped lower. A few clouds pushed in. The wind picked up. He crossed his fingers for rain. Maybe that would be his edge.

* * *

As they drew near the cave, Mage spotted Joe shinnying down from a red oak and hurried across the leafy forest floor to them. "Mister," he called out. "The boy is done gone."

Mage reined up. "The boy? Which boy?"

He pointed to Robert. "That one's brother."

Mage muttered an inaudible curse. He'd told William to stay put.

Inside, Laura put together a bag of grub for Mage while Robert switched his saddle and saddlebags to another pony, a deep-chested dun.

"He didn't say anything to anyone, Mage. He just rode out. I tried to stop him, but he didn't pay me any attention," Rachel said.

Mage picked up William's track easy enough. The pony's left front had a nick on the inside of the shoe, giving Mage an easy trail to follow. As he continued west toward Valley Springs, his concern for the boy's safety grew. If William continued his general direction, there was a good chance he would run across Shank Hughes and his noon meeting with the messenger from town.

Just before sundown, Mage reined up and grimaced at the ground. The sign was obvious. The track with the indention was mixed with those of another horse. There were scars in the hardpan indicating William's attempt to escape and Shank's short pursuit. From there, the tracks led southwest, William's pony trailing submissively behind.

A cold fear settling in his stomach, Mage looked up, peering into the dusk settling across the rolling countryside. By now, the two of them should have reached Black Draw. Would Shank force the boy to accompany them? Or would he leave him behind? He didn't figure the rustler would kill the boy, but he couldn't leave him behind to bring help. On the other hand, the rustler knew the state of the town, that there could be no effective pursuit for another week.

With a click of his tongue, he sent the dun southwest, for Black Draw.

Hughes squatted by the small fire and glared in triumph at the unconscious form of William Brewster sagging against the ropes binding him to the rugged trunk of an ancient water willow. His lips twisted in a sneer at the ugly bruises on the kid's face and the dried streak of blood on his chin. *Serves him right*, Hughes thought. *He shoulda known better than stampede the cattle out of the draw. I reckon he'll think twice before he does something like that again.* He shifted his gaze across the fire to Mustang Bill Lewis. "What's keeping Cooter?"

Lewis shrugged. "He said he was loading up some grub for us. He should be here by now. He said he reckoned on getting a pack horse to carry the extra grub."

Wrapping the handle of the coffeepot with a dirty cloth, Hughes poured himself another cup of coffee. "We don't need no extra grub. What we need is to push out soon as Lutie and Slim get here with the last two hundred head. And that's exactly what we're going to do even if Cooter ain't back."

Lewis rose from his squat and brushed the dust from his worn jeans. "What about that younker there? You got plans?"

"Naw," Hughes said. "Leave him be."

"He'll tell the town what we done, who we are." Lewis looked at Hughes in alarm.

Sneering, Hughes replied. "They'll know who we are. Besides, ain't nobody in town coming after us for another four or five days. By then we'll have the herd sold and be on the way to Mexico."

Lewis shoved his hat back and scratched head. "Five days? Why, it'll take us a week or more to get them to Houston."

With a sly grin, Hughes replied. "If we was going to Houston. I ran across a drifter today who told me that Shanghai Pierce is back west about forty miles pushing a herd to Kansas. We'll just ride over there and sell him these."

Frowning, Lewis glanced at the milling herd. "That's a heap of greenbacks for somebody on the trail to be carrying around with them."

"He ain't no somebody. I reckon Pierce picks up half his herd between South Texas and Kansas."

Lewis grimaced as he considered Hughes' new plan. He shook his head. "You always got some new angle, Shank. You sure do."

Mage had decided to delay the herd, but only after he pulled William Brewster out of the jam the boy had gotten himself into.

He had no idea what he would do until he saw what he was up against. All he knew was that somehow, he had to get the boy to safety, and without getting his own head blown off.

Chapter Eighteen

From inside the treeline, Mage spotted the small fire at Black Draw. Silhouetted figures moved about, but the distance was too great to tell what was going on. He had to move in closer.

Leaving his pony tied to a pine, he moved out on the prairie. There was no moon, but the stars cast a bluish glow over the rolling hills. Mage circled the small rises, hoping not to skyline himself. It took more time to cover the ground, but it eliminated the risk of being spotted.

Through the darkness off to his left came the whinny of horses and the bawling of calves, telling him that the rustlers were moving cattle. Whether into the draw or out, he had no way of knowing.

He dropped to his belly just below the crest of a small rise, fifty yards from the fire. His eyes grew cold, and his face went hard when he made out the limp form of William tied to the water willow. He suppressed the anger boiling in his blood.

The two shadows at the fire rose and stared north into the darkness. One of them gestured to the west, and they climbed on their horses, which were tied to nearby undergrowth and disappeared off to the west in the direction of the bawling cattle.

After they disappeared into the night, William raised his head and looked around. He had been faking unconsciousness. He struggled against the ropes binding him.

"That little devil," Mage muttered, proud of the boy's duplicity. He resisted the urge to call out to William. Rising to a crouch, he made a wide swing around the draw and dropped to his knees far back in the darkness behind the young man.

Tugging his hat down over his eyes, Mage buttoned his frock coat and turned up the collar, hoping to blend with the shadows stretching across the prairie.

He studied the camp for several seconds. To the west, the bawling of cattle continued. Were they moving the beeves in or out?

Without any further hesitation, he moved forward, six-gun in hand. With the boy exposed, gunfire was the last thing Mage wanted. He dropped to his belly behind a small rise less than ten yards from the fire and called softly. "Pssst! William!"

The young man froze. He turned his head. "Mr. Casebolt? Is that you?"

Mage jumped to his feet and sprinted to the tree. Three quick slashes, and the ropes fell away.

In a hushed voice, Mage said. "Can you run?"

William whispered. "Yes, sir."

"Then let's get out of here."

The boy jumped to his feet, then crumpled to the ground. He beat on his legs, muttering. "Cramped. That's all."

Mage helped him to his feet and with his arm around the youth's shoulder, hurried them in a half–trot back into the darkness toward the treeline where he had left his pony. At every step, he expected shouts of alarm.

After a hundred yards, he looked over his shoulder. His chest heaved, and he gasped for breath.

William pulled away. "I'm all right now."

"You sure?"

Breathing hard, the young man replied. "Yes, sir, Mr. Casebolt."

Mage glanced over his shoulder at the small patch of firelight in the middle of the darkness. Farther west, cattle were bawling and men were shouting. Shank was moving the herd out.

With William riding double, Mage angled across the prairie in the direction of the cave. Then he remembered the Circle L. He shouted over his shoulder. "You reckon the Circle L has any horses penned?"

"Got no idea."

But it was worth a try. If there were horses, he could send the boy back to the cave, and he could turn back to the herd. Might possibly save several hours, hours that he could turn to his advantage.

"We're going to take a look."

Thirty minutes later, he spotted a cluster of dark, bulky objects ahead. The Circle L, he guessed.

The buildings were dark, but there were animals moving about in the corrals. Within minutes, they had a pony saddled and tied next to Mage's dun at the hitch rail outside the chuckhouse. There was no grub inside, so they would have to do with what Laura Barton had packed that morning. With a lantern, Mage searched through the darkened buildings.

"What are we looking for, Mr. Casebolt?"

He grabbed a couple lariats and tossed them to William. "Anything that can help me."

"You? I want to go with you."

Mage looked at the young man whose face looked even younger in the pale light cast from the lantern. "No. I'm not going to get you hurt. You're riding back to the cave."

William set his jaw. "It's my pa's cattle they're rustling. I got the right to go."

Taking a threatening step toward the boy, Mage growled. "We ain't talking about rights, boy. We're talking about maybe getting yourself killed dead. No." He shook his head. "You're going back to the cave."

Swallowing hard, William fixed his eyes on Mage's. "Then I'll follow after you. I ain't going back to the cave."

There was no misreading of the determination in the young man's eyes. "I'll kick your tail."

"I don't care. I'll still follow."

Nodding to the chuckhouse, Mage threatened, "I might just tie you up and leave you in there."

"I'll get loose."

Mage knew when he was whipped. "You probably would. Well, I don't like it, and I'll probably be sorry for it, but all right."

A broad grin exploded across William's face, but Mage erased it immediately when he jammed his finger in the young man's chest. "But you do what I say, when I say, and do it fast. You understand?"

William nodded sheepishly.

With a weary shake of his head, Mage grunted. "Come on. Let's see what we can scrape up that we can use." In the storehouse, he ran across a half–full box of dynamite sticks. "Run outside and grab my saddlebags. And while you're out there, you might as well skedaddle over to the bunkhouse and grab yourself a couple blankets," he said to William as he sat the box of dynamite on the floor.

They packed a dozen or so sticks along with fuses in the saddlebags. In the main house, they discovered Winchesters and cartridges.

Before they rode out, Mage scribbled out a short note to John Madeley, itemizing the gear they had taken. Two minutes later, they were heading south across the prairie.

An hour later, Mage pulled up in a motte of scrub oak and dismounted.

William looked at him in surprise. "We stopping?"

A crooked grin played over Mage's lips. "We need some sleep."

"But, I ain't tired."

"Maybe not, boy, but I am. And whether you believe it or not, you need some rest too. I figure the rustlers will push 'til about sunrise, then take a break for a couple hours. Give the beeves a chance to rest up. Don't fret. We'll catch those old boys soon enough."

"You figured out what we're going to do?"

Mage screwed up his face in concentration. "Not exactly. I got a couple ideas sorta swimming around, but that's about all."

No sooner had Mage laid his head down on the blanket than the sun was peeking over the horizon. He sat up, trying to shake the cobwebs from his head. William was sleeping soundly, his arms flung wide and his mouth gaping open.

Mage grinned. For someone who wasn't tired, William sure was sleeping hard. He shook him. "Let's go, boy."

They snugged down the cinches, tied their blankets behind the cantle and swung onto the saddles. Breakfast was cold meat, hard biscuits, and flat water.

Leading the way due west, Mage explained what he had in mind. "They're moving south. We got to keep a sharp watch and spot them first. Shouldn't be any trouble for the ground is drying out from the rain, and the cows should be stirring up some dust."

William rode stiffly in the saddle, his eyes scanning the rolling hills before them. He nodded. "Then what?"

"I don't figure we can stop them." He patted the saddlebags. "But, with the dynamite, we ought to be able to scatter the herd good and proper. Make them spend a day or so just rounding the stock back up."

A broad grin spread over William's face, and he snickered. "Sure make Shank mad."

"Yeah. Reckon it will."

The boy's face grew somber. "But, once they gather the cows up, they'll start all over, won't they?"

Mage arched an eyebrow. "Wouldn't you? They don't have all the time in the world. Sooner or later, that sickness in town will be over. They'll be a heap of angry ranchers come boiling out of there like a swarm of bees."

"But, if we can keep slowing them down—"

With a wry laugh, Mage interrupted. "If we do, Shank'll come after us like a wild-eyed bronc. He's got no choice. He's on the run now, and he can't go back. He has one chance for a big score, and he'll jump on it like a duck on a junebug."

By mid-morning, they still had not seen sign of the rustled herd. Reining up on the crest of a small rise, Mage studied the countryside. The sun baked the prairie, pulling moisture from the soil in undulating waves that made the hills appear to be moving back and forth. "I can't figure not spotting them." He gestured to the south. "I don't know this country, but Houston is thataway, isn't it?"

Before the young man could reply, his horse spooked, rearing up and slamming his paws to the ground. The frightening hum of rattles filled the air like a thousand angry bees.

"Rattler," Mage shouted. "Back away."

"I'm trying," William shouted back, sticking tight in the saddle and hauling back on the reins. His startled pony responded and backed away.

The rattler remained coiled, his spade-shaped head waving back and forth, and his song of death spreading across the prairie.

"Let him be, boy. Let's give him all the room he wants." Mage rode another hundred yards and reined up, checking the area around him carefully.

William grinned weakly, his face pale. "I don't mind admitting it. Them snakes scare me no end."

"That's two of us, Two of us. Now, back to what we was talking about. Houston is south of us, isn't it?"

William shrugged. "I never been there, but that's what Pa said. Houston was south of our ranch—about six or seven days by wagon."

Stroking his chin, Mage grunted. "Well, then, I reckon if they didn't head south, they maybe they went west."

"They might of headed north. If they get across the Red River, nobody can touch them. At least, that's what Pa says. That's Indian Territory."

"Maybe. But north would keep them close to Valley Springs for two or three days. They want to get as far from the town as they can, and as soon as they can. South and west is the way to go. And they didn't go south."

Wheeling his dun about, Mage headed due north. "Somewhere up here, we'll cut their trail. They couldn't of just up and disappeared into thin air."

They spotted thin clouds of dust by noon. Reining up, Mage studied the wispy puffs of dust that spread for about a mile. "That has to be them." The rolling prairie stretched for miles in every direction. "They'll spot us if we get too close."

William frowned. "So how do we slow them down?"

Nodding farther west, Mage replied. "We'll ride ahead of them a few miles. I got a couple ideas."

"What kind?"

"I'm not sure. Let's see what the lay of the land is first."

Mid-afternoon, Mage and William pulled up at a small stream lined with ancient willows and looked over their back trail. The herd was about four or five miles back, appearing to be heading directly for them.

"Those boys are pushing the herd hard." He studied the terrain around them. "If I was them, I'd come through here. There's rises on either side. Let the stock spend the night here."

William looked at him expectantly.

Mage studied the area, glanced back toward the approaching herd, and nodded. "Now, here's what I have in mind. It'll be kind of chancy, but I'll guarantee you those boys won't forget it. Remember that rattler?"

Chapter Nineteen

The rustlers had no problems keeping the herd moving after sundown. The critters smelled the water, and there was no stopping them.

"Just find a spot above the cows to throw our blankets," Perl said, squirting a stream of tobacco juice into the muddy water.

Lewis and Cole took the first watch, nighthawking the herd while Perl boiled coffee and fried up some beef and beans.

All five cowpokes were worn to a nub, exhausted by the twenty or so hours in the saddle despite the two-hour break at sunrise. "How far you reckon we've come, Shank?"

The bearded rustler looked around at Slim Bachelor who was rolling out his blankets at the base of a large willow. "Maybe twelve miles. We still don't have no leader in them cows. We'd have made another three or four miles had we one."

Plopping down on his blankets and leaning back against the rugged bark of the water willow, Bachelor produced a bag of Bull Durham and proceeded to roll a cigarette. He nodded, knowing what Hughes meant. For any herd to trail proper, it needed a dominant animal to come to the front and stay there, refusing to let another animal get in front.

He glanced at a thick limb just over his head, making a note not to hit it when he stood up. He touched a match to his cigarette and grunted. "I remember a drive I made with the Robertson outfit out of Palo Pinto. We had an old brindle steer take over. That long-legged Mexican critter woulda took us twenty miles a day if the others could of kept up with him."

Perl looked up from the cooking fire. "Shame to kill one like that."

"Oh, Mr. Robertson didn't sell him. No sireee. He loaded that contrary piece of stringy meat in the train and hauled him all the way back to South Texas with the rest of his cowpokes for the next drive." He took a deep drag of the cigarette and blew the smoke into the darkening sky. "Why, wouldn't surprise me none if he was still using that old brindle."

Without warning, three deafening explosions rocked the night, lighting the sky with blinding flashes of light.

"What the—"

Before any of the rustlers could move, the bawling of frightening cows and the rumble of over four thousand hooves slamming into the ground rolled across the camp.

In the next instant, the peaceful waters of the serene little creek exploded into a froth as the herd stampeded over the camp.

No sooner had the flashes of light disappeared than

Hughes leaped for his saddle. He wheeled his horse about while he had one foot in the stirrup and was slinging his other leg over the saddle.

Bachelor jumped to his feet and banged his head into a limb, knocking himself back on his behind. A wave of blackness threatened him, but the penetrating fear of the runaway animals galvanized his frozen muscles. Somehow, he managed to climb into the tree fork above the backs of the rampaging cows where he promptly fainted.

With a yelp, Perl dropped the skillet and coffeepot and leaped for the nearest tree, dragging his foot out of the way just as the horns of the first terrified cow charged past.

Hughes dug his star rowels into the flanks of his black and leaned over the charging horse's neck, trying to find the point of the stampede. He veered to the left, out of the herd. If he fell, out here, he had a chance of rolling out of the way. Inside, he would be nothing but a damp spot in the ground.

Ahead, he spotted the dark bulk of the panicked leaders, racing blindly across the prairie. Trusting his horse's night instincts, Hughes pulled up beside the pounding animals. For a mile, he raced beside them. The herd was beginning to string out as the leaders pulled ahead.

Finally, the lead cows began to slow, and that was the signal for Hughes to start easing them in a wide swing, doubling back toward the creek and using the cows as a barrier to the ones behind.

Lewis appeared out of the darkness.

"Where's Lutie?" Hughes demanded.

"Out here somewhere. I lost track of him when them explosions come."

"What the blazes was that? Sounded like dynamite."

"I got no idea. One minute I was singing to the cows,

the next, those ornery critters was trying to stomp me in the ground."

An idea came to the rustler leader. "When you went back to the camp last night at the end of Black Draw, was that kid still there?"

"Yeah. He was asleep or passed out. Why?"

Shank ignored the question. "Find Lutie. Calm these beeves down. I'm going back to camp."

Lewis clicked his tongue. "I don't reckon there's a camp left. Them animals run smack over it."

Hughes paid him no attention. He knew who was behind the explosions. Somehow, that schoolteacher had got his hands on the dynamite. And as far as Hughes knew, the kid was in on it too. He tightened his hands on the reins and dug his heels wickedly into the black's flanks.

He was going to kill someone and enjoy every second of it.

Perl had pulled together a few branches and rebuilt the fire, by the light of which he searched for their gear. The skillet was still serviceable once he straightened the handle. The coffeepot had been stomped into a flat sheet of tin. The blankets were in remnants, and his saddle, as was Bachelor's, had been cut to pieces by the hooves of the runaway cows. Pieces of the pads hung from the saddle tree, the frame on which the saddle had been constructed.

He cursed. "I shoulda knowed," he muttered. "I was never cut out to be no rustler outlaw. I ain't going to fork this," he said, flinging the saddle into the darkness. "I'll ride bareback first."

A groan caught his attention. He looked around, but saw nothing. Then the groan came again. He looked up and spotted Bachelor draped over a fork in a willow. "You all right, Slim?"

The lanky cowpoke peered down through the branches. "I reckon. Head sure hurts."

A sharp pain hit Perl in the stomach, and a surge of bile boiled up his throat. That's when he realized that in the excitement, he had swallowed his wad of tobacco. He gagged, then growled at Slim. "Well, get your carcass down and help me sort things out here."

Bachelor grunted. He started down, then hesitated. He blinked his eyes, then shook his head, figuring the blow to his skull had him seeing things. He looked again. It was still there. Far off in the night, a camp fire. He frowned, wondering who it could be.

"Slim. You hear me. Get on down here," Cole yelled. "We got junk scattered everywhere." He gagged again.

A few minutes later, Hughes rode in, leading Perl's and Bachelor's ponies. He reined up, anger twisting his swarthy face as he surveyed the destruction about him. Perl and Bachelor cowered as he cursed. "You see anyone?"

"Not me. I was hanging on to that tree for dear life."

"Me neither," Bachelor said. "But I did spot a fire way off yonder to the south."

Hughes eyes grew wide. "A fire? Where?"

"Like I said, back south."

Twisting around in the saddle, Hughes stood in the stirrups. "I don't see no fire."

"Up yonder in the tree. That fork. You can see it from there."

Hughes stepped from the stirrup onto the first limb, then clambered up to the fork. He squinted into the night. A cruel grin twisted his thin lips when he spotted the small fire, but then turned into a frown. The schoolteacher wasn't dumb enough to build a fire right out in the open, unless he had done it deliberately, trying to draw Hughes and his boys over.

Or, it might just be a drifter. He dismissed that idea. Had it been a drifter, he would have come over to see what the commotion was all about.

Still, the fire bore looking into.

A few hundred yards north of the devastated camp, Mage and William sat astride their horses, watching the figures silhouetted against the fire.

William snickered. "We sure got them good."

A grin ticked up one edge of Mage's lips. "Don't laugh too much, boy. A joke can turn back on a man before he knows it. Let's just wait for the next part of the game."

"You reckon they spotted our fire?"

"We'll know sooner or later." They watched from a shallow bowl between two rises. Mage glanced around. Although the moon had not risen, the starlight was bright enough to show they were all alone. Back to the south, behind the dark bulk of the treeline along the meandering creek, cows bawled and distant shouts echoed through the night.

"They're doing something," William whispered. "Ain't that them mounting up?"

Moments later, three horses rode in front of the fire and disappeared into the darkness.

The young boy chuckled. "Sure wish I could be there."

"We got other work to do. You got your dynamite?"

"Right here in my pocket."

"All right. Let's us swing wide around the herd. This time they won't have as much luck hauling those critters in. They're spooky now. Next one will send them clean up to Canada. Now remember, soon as the commotion starts over yonder at the camp, chunk the dynamite."

Hughes pulled up a couple hundred yards from the fire. The small flames flared from time to time, casting a yellow glow on the willow trees overhead.

He shucked his handgun and motioned for Bachelor and Perl to swing around either side of the camp. After a few minutes, he eased forward and halted just beyond the light cast by the flickering fire. There were no ponies in sight, but he figured they had picketed the animals in some graze.

His eyes grew narrow when he spotted the bulk of two bedrolls a few feet from the small fire. He glanced around suspiciously. How could any jasper sleep through those explosions and the subsequent stampede even if it had occurred over a mile away?

He eased forward, squinting into the shadows. One of the bedrolls moved. He studied it a moment. Sure enough. Looked like someone was shifting his feet around.

At that moment, he caught movement beyond the camp. Bachelor and Perl. Giving a soft whistle, he eased his pony across the creek and into the camp as his partners entered from the other side.

The figures in the blankets didn't stir, and their heads were covered. He frowned, suddenly wary. What if these jaspers had the sickness?

Dismounting, Hughes crept to one of the bedrolls, motioning Perl and Bachelor to do the same. He cocked his sixgun and nudged the blanket with his toe.

The bedroll stirred. A sound like a moving arm against the blanket reached him. He tightened his finger on the trigger and reached for a corner of the blanket.

Perl followed his example. "Now," Hughes shouted, jerking the blanket away.

A dozen infuriated rattlesnakes came after him.

"Yaaaah!" Hughes cried. He frantically stumbled back, emptying his revolver into the mass of writhing, hissing rattlers, completely oblivious to the fact that Bachelor and Perl were scrambling for their lives.

At that moment, the campfire exploded, sending sparks and coals a hundred feet into the dark sky.

Hughes spun and grabbed for his black, but the horse had shied from the shouts and gunfire. His hair standing on end, the rustler leader chased his horse into the night.

Perl grabbed the mane of his pony, which bolted and dragged the old man through the creek and onto the prairie. Cursing the animal, Perl twisted his fingers in the mane and shouted for it to stop, but the frightened horse had the bit in his teeth and was not to be halted.

Perl felt his fingers slip. Fear knotted his stomach when he realized how close he was to the pounding hooves. He'd seen hombres who had the misfortune of falling under horses. Maybe he could throw himself aside.

Suddenly, the mane slithered through his fingers. He opened his mouth to cry out, but the knee of the frightened pony caught his chin and sent him spinning, saving his life except for the leg the pony's hind feet struck, shattering his shinbone into a dozen pieces.

Bachelor swung a long leg over the back of his sorrel and slammed his heels into the pony's flanks. The startled animal leaped forward, racing through the willows. Bachelor glanced back. He never saw the limb that struck the side of his head, somersaulting him over the rear of his horse.

He slammed to the ground, his head bent at an unnatural angle.

Across the prairie, Mage waited. He peered into the darkness to his left, but it had swallowed William and his pony completely. As soon as the gunfire commenced, Mage touched a match to the fuses of the two sticks of dynamite in his hand.

He drove the dun forward across the creek and hurled

the sticks as far as he could. Far to his left, he spotted a fiery arc spinning through the air.

He jerked around when he heard an explosion from across the prairie in the camp with the rattlesnakes.

Seconds later, three more explosions rocked the prairie, and a thousand head of cattle scattered like a handful of dust tossed into a stiff wind.

Mage pulled up back north a few hundred yards, where he and William were to meet. A few minutes later, the soft clop of hooves broke the silence. "Mr. Casebolt. That you?"

"Over here."

William was in a jovial mood. "We sure took care of them, didn't we?"

With a grin of his own, Mage said, "Looks that way, but best we keep an eye 'til sunup. We'll move north and grab some shuteye. Come morning, we'll have a better idea of what we got done. By the by, boy. What was that explosion in the camp? Sounded like dynamite to me."

William looked around at him. In the starlight, Mage saw the smug look on the young man's face. "Yes, sir. I rigged a stick of dynamite on a willow limb over the fire and hooked it to the blanket so when they moved the blanket, the stick would fall into the fire." He hesitated. "Sure worked good too, didn't it?" His grin grew wider.

Mage chuckled. "Yeah, boy, it sure worked good. Now, let's us go find a spot to rest up."

Chapter Twenty

Cowboys hate to walk. Rather than take a couple dozen steps, most opt to climb aboard their ponies. So, Hughes was furious when he had to traipse a couple miles before he could lay a hand on the reins of his spooked horse. His arches throbbed, and his throat was like sandpaper. He cursed the animal in one breath, the schoolteacher in the next, and the lack of water with the next.

To add insult to injury, when Hughes tried to mount, the black shied, dragging the cursing rustler after him, one foot caught in the stirrup, the other digging into the ground. He yanked on the reins, jerking the black's head toward him viciously. "You best calm down, horse. Elsewise, I'll blow that empty head of yours apart even if I gotta walk fifty miles."

Finally, he managed to swing onto the saddle, every

muscle taut with fury and frustration. Yanking the black's head around, he dug his spurs in, taking out his anger on the hapless animal.

The black laid his ears back and rolled his eyes.

Back at the camp, Hughes halted in the middle of the creek. His weathered face twisted in anger, He cursed when he spotted the lifeless body of Slim Bachelor sprawled on the bank. He looked around the devastated camp. He saw no sign of the rattlers or of Perl. "No telling where the old man be," he muttered, turning and heading south to his camp.

"Blast that schoolteacher," the rustler muttered sometime later. He had ridden a couple miles across the prairie, spotting the dark bulk of a handful of cows but no sign of Cole or Lewis.

The darkness on the eastern horizon began to move back to the west as the new day approached. His eyes red-rimmed for lack of sleep, Hughes glared malevolently at the false dawn.

Suddenly, a distant shout behind him broke the silence of the early morning. He squinted into that gauzy gray haze between night and day. A single rider headed his way. He leaned forward and strained his eyes.

Cole.

Hughes leaned back in his saddle, wondering about Lewis. Had he been caught up in the stampede? The rustler leader shook his head in disgust. He felt sorry for himself. If it wasn't for bad luck, he'd have no luck at all.

Moments later, the old man pulled up beside Hughes and shrugged. "We got us one big mess here. Them critters is scattered all over five counties. The Devil himself ain't going to pull them back together."

Hughes cursed. "Where's Bill?"

Cole hooked a thumb over his shoulder. "Gone to Houston and places south," he said. "He rode out a while back. We tried to turn the critters, but they just kept on agoing. That's when Bill just shook his head and said he was pulling foot out of here."

By now, the sun had risen.

Hughes looked around. A few head of cows stood hipshot within his sight. Maybe twenty, he guessed. Sure not enough to get hanged over.

Cole interrupted his thoughts. "What now, Shank?"

The rustler leader snorted and gave Cole a wry grin. "Well, they can't get us for rustling. We can always claim we was just moving them cows to fresh graze. They wouldn't believe us, but I don't reckon they'd go so far to hang us. Still, I'm figuring the smart move is to hightail it out of here. Go somewhere else in another state and start over."

"That what you're going to do?"

Hughes peered back to the east. "Just as soon as I take care of some unfinished business," he said.

Cole nodded slowly and glanced over his shoulder. "Personally, I always did want to see Mexico and them pretty little *senoritas*."

A few miles to the northwest, Mage had slept in snatches the remainder of the night, awakening each time with a start, his fingers tightly around the butt of his Colt.

His dun grazed peacefully. Mage relaxed. If there were any horses around for a mile or so, the dun would pick them up. Still, best to keep a sharp watch.

As the sun rose, he built a small fire, doing his best to keep it smokeless.

He nudged William with the toe of his boot. "Grab some grub and tighten the cinch. Best we push on out."

Fifteen minutes later, they were swinging west, hoping to come in from a direction the rustlers wouldn't be watching although had he been one of them, at this point in time, he'd be watching all points of the compass.

Gradually, they started a southward swing. Mage had an idea where the first camp was, but in the vast emptiness of the Texas prairie, landmarks were hard to come by, so a jasper had to rely on his own sense of direction.

"Hey, look, Mr. Casebolt. Over there. Ain't that a horse?"

Sure enough, a half-mile or so across the prairie, a horse was staring at them. Its reins appeared to be dragging the ground, but at such a distance, it was impossible to tell.

As they drew closer, the horse tried to shy away, but his reins had tangled in some scrub undergrowth. "Easy, boy," Mage whispered as he leaned forward and grabbed the reins. "Take it easy."

"You think it's one of the rustlers'?"

"Seems logical," Mage said.

"Wonder where the rider is?"

The scrub around them was empty. In the blue sky overhead, a few hawks circled. Then far to the east, Mage made out larger shapes circling. He glanced at William. The boy spotted the buzzards at the same time.

"You think that's the rider over there?"

Mage touched his heels to his pony's flanks. "We're going to find out."

As they drew near, Mage unholstered his Colt and studied the countryside around them. A jasper can never be too careful. Then he spotted another column of circling buzzards farther east, above a line of trees, the site of their false camp from the night before.

"Look," William said. "The buzzards are after something over there." He pointed to a couple buzzards waddling around behind the crest of a small rise. Only their heads were visible.

Clicking his tongue, Mage urged his pony into a gallop. Startled, the buzzards lumbered away, flapping their large wings, slowly taking to the air.

Beyond the rise, they found an old man sprawled face down in the grass.

"Is he dead?"

Mage rolled the man over and laid his hand on his chest. "Nope. He's breathing pretty regular." He grimaced at the swollen jaw and the fresh blood seeping from the man's mouth. Whoever the hombre is, he came out on the short end of the stick, Mage told himself. He noted the man's leg seemed twisted at an awkward angle. He touched his fingers to the unconscious man's shin, and a sharp gasp of pain burst from the man's lips.

The old man's eyes were bare slits. Through parched, bloody lips, he muttered, "Busted, ain't it?"

"Sure looks that way, partner. What the Sam Hill you doing out here anyway? You one of Shank's boys?"

Perl hurt too bad to lie. "Yeah. Took a fool chance and look what I got for it."

Mage eyed the circling buzzards at the creek. "Reckon you can stay on a horse for a mile or so?"

The old man nodded slowly. "I reckon."

Mage relieved the old man of his handgun and knife. All he found when he searched Perl was a bag of Bull Durham and a single gold coin, both of which he left in the old man's pockets.

He glanced up at William. "Give a hand with him. Then ride on to the camp on the creek. See what those other buzzards are after."

Together, they slid Perl into his saddle. The leather-tough old man tried to clench his teeth, but his jaws didn't mesh properly. He screamed, but it only came out a muffled moan. Each jolting step sent shards of pain shooting through the old man's body. He gripped the saddle horn so tightly his knuckles turned white.

Even before he reached the creek, Mage spotted William standing motionless, staring at the dead man on the ground. The young man looked up as Mage and Perl drew near. He shook his head.

Under his breath, Mage muttered a curse. He glanced around the clearing. "You check for snakes, boy?"

William grinned. "Real good before I even got down."

Mage wasn't convinced. He remained in the saddle while he scanned the area again. "Well, I sure hope those fellers are gone."

Together, they helped Perl to the ground, after which Mage set his leg while William used his knife to start digging out a grave for the dead man.

Perl watched as they buried his one–time partner. "Slim was a good hand with cows. Hate he come to such a bad end."

Mage glanced at the pain-wracked old man. "His choice."

"Yep, reckon you're right there." His words came out between gasps of pain.

Brushing the dirt from his hands, Mage looked around. "Now, let's us build a travois. Won't be no easy trip back to town, but at least you can lay down," he told Perl.

"What about the cows and the other rustlers?" William asked. "Hadn't we best look after them instead of wasting time on him?"

With a chuckle, Mage laid out the travois poles on the ground. "Well, boy, from the looks of things, them cows is scattered from Heaven to Hades. Here we got two of the rustlers accounted for. That leaves three, and even if they ride from sunup to sundown, it'll take 'em a week to gather enough stock for the gamble to be profitable. Nope, I reckon them that's smart enough has done lit a shuck out of here."

William dropped an armload of green branches and began lashing them to the travois poles. "I sure hope you're right, Mr. Casebolt."

Mage tied a branch to the poles. "I do too."

When they finished the travois, Mage lashed the poles to the saddle on Perl's horse.

Shank Hughes watched as Lutie Cole turned his little mare about and touched his spurs to her flanks. Houston–bound, the rail-thin old cowpoke never looked back.

Hughes turned east. His reputation in Valley Springs was ruined. If they arrested him, he'd probably be the guest at a necktie party, an honor that he would just as soon decline. But, he had one problem to handle before he pulled out. One problem he would enjoy taking care of—revenge.

He wanted the schoolteacher.

Chapter Twenty-one

T ravel with a travois was slow. Mage's small party spent the night at the Circle L and reached Valley Springs about noon the following day.

Doc Shelby figured that the sickness had run its course enough that Cooter Perl would not contract the illness, and if he did, it served him right for trying to take advantage of the situation in which the community had found itself.

As a precaution, however, the doctor insisted Mage and William back away a fair distance as he, Frank Brewster, William's pa, and Sheriff Swink, took Perl off their hands.

The two sat astride their horses, looking down at the small collection of townspeople as Mage explained what had taken place.

Swink plopped down on the boardwalk in front of the general store and wiped the sweat from his forehead. "I'd ride along with you, Mage, but I'm still weak as pond water. I got to stop every few minutes and rest up."

"Nothing for you to worry about, sheriff. William and me, we're riding back to the cave. We'll come in tomorrow and the next 'til Doc tells us it's safe for us."

Brewster cleared his throat. "Schoolteacher, now them rustlers is gone, you can take those kids to our place. Doc says we should be out of here in a couple more days."

Mage and William rode out of Valley Springs along the east road. "Uh, oh," Mage said when he spotted the dark clouds rolling in from the southeast. "Looks like more weather coming."

Grimacing, the boy grumbled. "And we ain't got no slickers either."

They were still a couple miles from the ranch when Mage spotted the rain racing across the prairie toward them like a gray veil. He tugged his hat down on his head. "Here it comes."

It struck hard, soaking them instantly. At first the sandy ground soaked up the water thirstily, but within minutes, tiny rivulets of runoff water cut through the sand to reach the ditch along the side of the road.

Soon the rivulets were tiny streams, then cascades.

"There's the ranch," William called out, pointing to a cluster of desolate–looking buildings ahead. Rain lashed the rooves. A few head of cows and horses stood around, heads drooping against the pounding rain. Mage spotted some of the smarter ponies in the barn, but as they drew near the horses bolted from the corral.

Reining up at the main house, Mage said, "Let's see what kind of grub we can scrape up for the kids. It'll be nigh on dark by the time we reach the cave."

The storm filled the ranch house with shadows. William

lit a lantern. He looked around in surprise. Cabinet doors hung open; the contents of drawers had been dumped on the floor; and boxes of cartridges had been broken open.

Mage clicked his tongue. "Looks like those old boys took whatever they could find."

William clenched his teeth. "I'd like to shoot them for doing this. This ain't—I sure wish I could get my hands on them."

"Take it easy, boy. Nothing done around here that can't be put back. I reckon your ma will have this place spic and span before you can whistle Dixie."

"Reckon you're right, Mr. Casebolt. It just makes me mad enough to bite a nail in two." Suddenly, his grin faded.

"What's wrong, boy?"

William didn't answer. He rushed into the pantry and retrieved his father's moneybox. He flipped it open and stared into it. He clenched his teeth. "Gone." He looked at Mage in disbelief. "It's all gone. They stole all of Pa's money." He brushed past Mage. "We got to run them down. They got Pa's money."

"Easy, son. Easy. How you going to run them down? The only one you got a handle on is that jasper back in town. He didn't have but a gold coin on him. He sure isn't going nowhere. He'll keep 'til we get back. Now, you and me, we got to get to the kids."

They rode out with bags of canned goods, a salted ham and tarps. Each had also slipped a box of cartridges in the saddlebags.

Water filled the shallow ruts of the road.

The rustlers had fled, but there were still Comanche about, so Mage rode with one eye constantly searching the horizon.

Gradually, the rain tapered off to a steady drizzle. Just

before sundown, Mage spotted the tree line. They kept their ponies at a steady lope. "Think you can find the cave in the dark?"

William didn't answer for a moment. He studied the sagging limbs and drooping leaves in the forbidding shadows of the forest looming before him. He shook his head. "No, sir. All I know is that a good piece in there, you'll find a big valley. I reckon we'd have to ride along the rim to find the cave."

Riding out a couple days earlier, Mage had studied his back trail. But in the dark, he couldn't spot the landmarks, so he couldn't afford to take them too deep into the forest for fear of wandering off the trail. More than once, he'd found himself lost in the middle of the hardwood forests back east, and he well remembered the feeling of hopelessness that flooded over him.

The pine and oak forest allowed some protection against the drizzle, but not enough to allow their clothes to dry. A wet, miserable night lay ahead. At least, they didn't have to face one of those Texas Northers he'd heard so much about.

A hundred yards into the forest, they came upon a windfall created when a dead pine fell, splintering several smaller pines and lodging in the fork of a great oak. Over the years, berry vines covered the windfall, creating a hollow beneath the pine in which a man could stand. Mage remembered riding past it on the way out.

He reined up.

"Trouble?"

"Naw. I remember this place. This is as good a spot as any to spend the night. It's too dark to ride on. That dead pine and the vines above block out some of the rain. We'll toss a tarp over it. If nothing else, it'll keep most of the water off us."

Within minutes, a cheery fire burned beneath the windfall. "Not too big," Mage said to the young man. "We don't want to burn our house down."

William laughed. "Some house."

Mage opened two cans of beans and slid them into the coals. "Few minutes and you can sink your teeth into a thick steak and chase it with a cold bee–milk."

William grinned. "Funny looking steak."

"Just use your imagination, son. Just use your imagination."

Despite exercising his imagination, the water from the canteen didn't taste like milk, and the beans tasted nothing like steak, but they were hot and filling. And later, when William slid into his bedroll, he felt a sense of warmth and comfort. Overhead, the drizzle continued to patter against the tarp.

During the night, a faint sound awakened Mage. He lay motionless, staring in the darkness as the embers glowed.

He strained his ears, but all he heard was the rain dripping on the tarp. He figured it was just his mind playing tricks. He rolled over and pulled the blanket about his neck, and then he heard a faint murmur.

He sat up and squinted into the darkness, listening carefully. *Sounded like a voice, but who? Out here in the middle of the night?* Mage decided it was probably a rabbit or maybe a distant yelp of a coyote.

He lay back, wondering about the children. *Don't be an idiot. No one is going to be out on a night like this.*

Mage dozed. Sometime later, his eyes popped open to a distant sound like a cough drifting through the darkness. As he listened, the sound came once again. He peered at their ponies, but the darkness was too complete to discern the animals.

No sounds reached his ears from the animals. They

seemed frozen in place. In his mind's eye, he saw them staring into the darkness.

Mage slid silently from his blankets just as William whispered, "What's wrong?"

In the faint glow of the blinking coals, William appeared as an indistinct outline. "Just stay here and be quiet," Mage replied softly. "You got your saddlegun?"

"Right beside me."

"Well, then, you keep tight hold of it. I'll be back directly."

Mage had forgotten just how complete the darkness within a forest could be on an overcast night. He jerked to a halt at the end of the windfall. Before him, he saw nothing, not even his hand at the tip of his nose.

He backed up. "I don't reckon I'm going anywhere, boy. It's darker than the inside of a cow out there."

"What's out there?"

Mage shook his head. "I'm not sure. You go on back to sleep. It'll be morning soon."

"You going back to sleep?"

"No. I'll sit up."

"Me too. I ain't sleepy."

Mage suppressed a chuckle. Moments later, he heard the regular breathing of the young man as he slept.

As the first gray light of morning drifted through the forest, Mage tossed more wood on the fire. He peered through the tangle of vines surrounding the windfall, curious as to the sounds of the night before. He shrugged. Probably nothing more than a fertile imagination.

While they were squatting in front of the fire sipping coffee, a distant cry sounded from the depths of the forest.

Mage shucked his Colt and nodded to William's saddlegun. "Over there," he said. "Get behind the roots. I'll be over here."

They worked into the thick brush at either end of the windfall, and waited.

The cry came again, this time closer.

Easing through the tangle of underbrush, Mage peered in the direction of the cry. Thick shadows lay across the open floor of the forest, but within moments, faint strokes of sunlight began sweeping the darkness aside.

Suddenly, his eyes picked up movement at the edge of a shadow. A dark figure staggered a few steps, then fell. It lay motionless a few seconds, then struggled to its feet and lunged forward, managing to cover several more feet before falling.

Keeping his eyes on the figure, Mage called William. "Over here, boy."

"What do you see?"

"Not too sure. Someone out there. Acts like he's hurt, but we can't take a chance. You move in here with that saddlegun. I'll go meet him. He tries anything, you shoot."

William gulped. "I–I ain't never shot no one."

"That makes us even. I ain't never been killed, so don't let me start now, you hear?"

The young man forced a weak grin. "Yes, sir. Don't worry."

Mage laid his hand on William's arm. "I'm not."

The leafy forest floor was spongy and quiet. Mage eased through the trees toward the slight figure who had sat up and was leaning against the thick bole of an ancient loblolly pine, his chin resting on his chest. When Mage was fifty feet from the tree, the man looked around.

Mage gaped. He mouthed the word, "Joe." And then aloud, he called out. "Joe? Joe? Is that you?" The old man frowned, his dark face blending with the shadows. "Joe, is that you?"

A shaft of sunlight burst through the leafy canopy overhead, illuminating the old man's face. "Mister? That you? That really be you?"

Holstering his sixgun, Mage hurried to the old man, at the same time shouting over his shoulder. "William. Come arunning."

Joe pushed away from the tree and fainted.

Together, they half-carried, half-dragged the worn-out old man back to the windfall where they laid him on Mage's bedroll and wrapped William's dry blanket around him.

Mage bent to wash the old man's face and recoiled when he saw the bruises on Joe's face and swelling about the old man's eyes and lips. He cursed to himself.

At the same time, William poured some steaming coffee in a tin cup and cooled it with a shot of water and handed it to Mage.

He held Joe's head and touched the cup to the old man's swollen and split lips. "Here."

Eagerly, Joe sipped the coffee.

"Easy, old man. Not too fast. We got plenty."

After a few moments, Joe tried to open his eyes. One was swollen shut. The other, he managed to open to a slit. "I mighty glad to find you, mister. We got trouble."

A sudden fear knotted in Mage's stomach. He shot a glance at William. "What kind of trouble?"

"A man come looking for you. Says you got payback coming. He tried to make us tell where you was, but we couldn't say."

Mage eyed the old man's battered face. "He did that?"

Joe nodded. "Then I snuck out to find you."

"Who is that hombre? You know?" Mage had the sinking feeling he knew the answer, but he wanted to hear it from Joe.

"He the one what shoots you."

Shank Hughes!

Chapter Twenty-two

Mage stared wordlessly at Joe, cold fear driving knives into his heart. Shank Hughes! Mage figured he was high-tailing it out of the county. The last thing he expected was for the rustler to retaliate on the children.

Joe struggled to sit up. Mage held him down, but the old man threw off Mage's hand. His voice was slow and heavy, weighted with weariness and fear. "We gots to get back. That man be crazy. He going to hurt one of them childs."

Mage glanced at William, noting the alarm in the young man's eyes and knowing the same fear shown in his own. He turned back to Joe. "How about you? How'd you get out?"

"I hopes I made him figure I done fall in one of those holes back in the cave tunnels, but I come out in back of the cave."

A surge of hope flooded through Mage's veins. "The back of the cave? You say there's a back way into the cave?"

Joe nodded.

The gambler studied the old man, wondering if he should go in through the front of the cave or take a chance on Joe being able to find the back entrance in his condition. "Think you can find the way back in?"

The old man gave a single nod. "It be dark when I comes out." He hesitated. A look of determination filled his eyes and he nodded again, this time surely. "I can find it."

"I hope so. A heap is counting on it." Mage went to his saddlebags and dug through his gear. With a nod of satisfaction, he found exactly what he was looking for.

William frowned. "What kinda rig is that, Mr. Casebolt?"

Mage removed his frock coat. "One that might very well save someone's life, son. Mine."

Shank Hughes glared at the defiant young man facing him. "Don't you lie to me, boy."

Robert Brewster swallowed the lump of fear in his throat. He scrubbed at the tears in his eyes. "I ain't lying. You saw for yourself the hole the old man fell in."

"Yeah, but I didn't see no body."

"Nobody did. Those holes are deep, probably too deep to see all the way to the bottom."

Hughes shifted his gaze from the frightened boy to the tunnel down which Joe had fled. Cursing to himself, he replayed the scene in his head, the old man's dash for the tunnel, the hasty shot Hughes tossed off at him, the slug striking the corner of the tunnel and ricocheting, followed by the old man's screams.

Hughes had rushed to the hole. Joe was nowhere to be

seen, but his hat lay on the ground near the rim of the shaft dropping deep into the bowels of the earth. Joe's footprints were obvious. He was the only one with brogans, and the tracks led right in.

Later, doubts arose in Hughes' mind. Now, he wanted to know for sure.

"Build me a torch, boy," he told Robert.

The young man shrugged. "What with? We ain't got no coal oil. Ain't nothing else going to burn worth a plugged nickel."

With an angry growl, Hughes viciously backhanded the boy, sending him spinning to the ground. "Blast you, I said get me a torch, and don't argue none about it."

The women and children looked on as Robert wound some rags around a dry branch. Without coal oil or fuel of some sort, even the youngest of the children knew the torch would only give off a dim glow, certainly not one bright enough to light up the shaft.

Joe paused, staring at the leaf-covered ground sloping away before him. Patches of sunlight dotted the slope, revealing a trail of disturbed leaves that led several yards down the hill to a tangle of wild huckleberries and dewberry vines. The old man looked around, a frown on his dark face. Slowly, he nodded. "This be the place, mister. Down yonder is where I comes out of the cave."

Mage slid down the hill and squatted in front of the rear entrance. He studied the small opening. He would have to go in on hands and knees. His heart thudded in his chest as he broke out into a cold sweat.

Missouri came back to haunt him—the tornado, the panic he fought for two days after the building caved in, trapping him and two others in the debris. Unable to move, he lay motionless as dirt sifted through the cracks, filling his ears, pressing against his cheeks. He remembered the fear that he would be buried alive, suffocated before rescuers reached him.

The other two died the first night. During the second day, Mage could hear the gases at work inside their swelling bodies.

Now, he stared into the narrow, dark tunnel. He closed his eyes and swallowed the copper taste of fear. His voice cracked when he spoke. "How far before it opens up?"

"A piece. Hard to remember, but when it opens, you stay to this side," he said, gesturing to Mage's left. The other side has gots holes that drop into the ground."

Mage stared into the darkness. He closed his eyes, trying to suppress the panic threatening what little self-control he still possessed.

He tried to push Missouri aside, the darkness over his face, the suffocating closeness. He caught himself and rose quickly to his feet, his teeth clenched. He forced himself to study the forest about them. "The mouth of the cave is yonder way," he said, pointing southeast. Give me some time." He jabbed a twig in the middle of a small patch of sunlight. "When the shadow reaches about here," he explained, laying his forefinger on the ground, "start tossing whatever you can at the mouth of the cave to get his attention. I'll come in behind him."

"What if we're too late?" William asked.

Mage forced a reassuring grin. "Don't worry. If I get there early, I'll wait until you get his attention." He took a deep breath. He hoped they couldn't see just how uncertain he was. The truth was, Mage wasn't even sure if he had courage enough to even stick his head inside the tunnel.

Hughes stood at the lip of the shaft, holding the flickering torch above the mouth of the gaping abyss. The dim light penetrated the darkness only a few feet. He cursed. "Can't see a blasted thing down there."

Robert watched warily from a short distance. His eye had swollen from the blow he had taken from Hughes.

Taking a step back, Hughes dropped the torch into the shaft, craning his neck to peer over the rim, but within seconds, the flickering fire disappeared. He remained motionless, his head cocked to one side listening for the torch to strike bottom.

After several seconds, he backed away, muttering. "Ain't nobody could live through a fall like that." If he did fall, he told himself. He cursed, wishing he could see the body.

He shot a malevolent look at Robert. "What the blazes you staring at, boy? Get back in there with the women and the other brats."

Rachel and Laura had managed to keep the children calm despite the fear Shank Hughes had put in them.

Hughes studied the tunnel. Maybe he should put a joker in the deck just in case he needed it.

Mage waved Joe and William in the direction of the cave entrance. "Get ready over there. I'm going in."

With a brief nod, William led the way. Joe tagged behind. Mage watched them trudge off, wishing he were in their shoes. He closed his eyes and drew several deep breaths. Then before he could reconsider, he dropped to his hands and knees and plunged into the small tunnel.

The tunnel was dark as midnight on Boot Hill. He closed his eyes, using his hands to pick up any change in direction of the tunnel. His hat scraped dirt from the top of the cave, spilling some down his neck and reminding him of the horror of the imprisoned feeling he had lived through once before.

He felt as if he were trapped in a towsack, his arms

pinned to his side. He paused, and his muscles began to spasm. Clenching his teeth, he continued crawling, forcing his trembling muscles to propel him forward. His breathing grew rapid and shallow, but he persisted, reminding himself over and over that somewhere ahead, the tunnel opened into a larger one. Seconds seemed like hours, but Mage persisted, one hand in front of the other, his shoulders scraping the tunnel wall on either side.

Without warning, his right shoulder did not scrape the wall. He jerked to a halt, a lump of fear in the pit of his stomach. Gingerly he reached out, feeling for the wall, but touched nothing but air. Swinging his arm slowly backward, his fingers touched the wall about a foot behind his shoulders.

He had reached the cave!

A wave of relief washed over him. He grinned, grateful to be free of the narrow confines. Not even the darkness of the cave and the danger of the unseen shafts could suppress the smile that came to his lips.

He shoved his right hand forward, pushing his fingers through the dirt before bringing his left up beside it. Then he repeated the steps over again.

Within a few feet, his right hand touched air. With a start, he jerked it back and leaned against the wall of the cave. When his breathing slowed, he reached out his hand again, touching the rim of the shaft, measuring its proximity in regard to the wall of the cave.

Gingerly, he crawled past the opening, then continued forward once again.

The cave seemed to be turning back to his left, and abruptly, the glow of light came from the end of the tunnel. At the same time, the chilling buzz of a rattlesnake ripped through the shadows.

Mage froze, peering into the semi-darkness in an effort

to locate the snake. Best he could tell, the snake was near the opposite wall. He guessed that he had just disturbed it, and the serpent was warning him not to come closer.

Rising to his feet, Mage leaned against the wall. If he miscalculated on the location of the rattler, he'd sooner it took a lick at his boots than his shoulders.

Moving slowly, he side-stepped along the wall, praying that Joe was right about all the shafts being against the far wall. He began to breath easier as the hum of rattles fell behind. He turned his attention back to the light at the end of the tunnel.

Hughes heard peculiar noises coming from the front of the cave. He eased to the bend and peered around the corner. A thick mat of vines covered the entrance. Even as he watched, the noise came again, like something falling.

He moved closer to the entrance, sixgun in hand, half expecting the schoolteacher to come riding in. Instead, he spotted a broken branch in the middle of the trail. With a shrewd grin, he holstered his sixgun. Nothing but a limb busted off an old tree up above. As he watched, two more limbs fell.

He studied the broken branches. A slow grin twisted in thin lips. You ain't so smart, schoolteacher, he told himself as he returned to the fire inside the cave.

Mage looked around the corner of the tunnel as Hughes squatted by the fire and poured some coffee. The women and children watched him silently, their fear of him evident in their eyes.

Studying the situation, Mage decided to wait until Hughes returned to the mouth of the cave once again before making his move. If he remained in the shadows along the wall, he might reach the wagon where he could await Hughes' return, and catch the rustler by surprise.

After a few minutes, Hughes poured his coffee on the fire and rose to his feet. He took a step toward the mouth of the cave, then hesitated, glancing back at the tunnel in which Mage crouched.

Mage jerked back and pressed up against the wall of the cave. He flexed his fingers about the butt of his Colt as footsteps approached. The rocks in the wall felt like knives in his back.

Then the footsteps stopped. For long seconds, the silence of the cave rang in Mage's ears. Then the footsteps moved away.

Mage relaxed. Hughes was heading for the mouth of the cave. Now was the time to slip over to the wagon. He eased toward the corner of the tunnel. He peered into the shadows. Hughes had disappeared. Mage guessed the rustler had slipped up to the mouth of the cave.

He stepped forward quickly, too quickly. His boot snagged on a cord stretched ankle high, causing him to stumble forward in the middle of a racket of tin cans that sounded like a dozen shotguns in the silence of the cave.

Mage scrambled to his feet, glancing down at the cord strung across the entrance to the tunnel. Several empty cans were fastened to it.

Before he could react, a self-satisfied voice halted him. "Well, well, look what we got here. The schoolteacher."

Mage jerked around and stared into the muzzle of Hughes' sixgun. He started to bring his own revolver up, but the threat in Hughes' voice stopped him. "One more move, and you're buzzard food."

Behind Hughes, Rachel stared at them, her hands pressed against her lips.

"That's it, schoolteacher. Now, drop that sixgun."

Straightening, Mage tossed the revolver aside. In the next instant, he shot his left arm out, and a hide-out Derringer popped out from his sleeve, the two-hole muzzle less than a foot from Hughes' head.

The move caught the rustler by surprise. Then he saw the small pistol. "Now, ain't that cute?"

Mage sneered. "May be cute, but those two little holes will kill you as dead as that .44 you're toting."

It was a standoff.

For several seconds, the two stared at each other.

Finally, Hughes lowered his sixgun and slid it into his holster. "All right, schoolteacher. Now what?"

Mage frowned, surprised at the rustler's sudden capitulation. At that moment, Rachel shouted. Mage glanced her direction, giving Hughes the split second he needed.

Like a striking snake, he grabbed Mage's hand with the Derringer and jerked. At the same time, he threw a straight right that caught Mage stumbling forward.

Lights exploded in Mage's head, and he fell backwards, the Derringer flying into the shadows.

Rachel's shrill voice cut the darkness like a bolt of lightning. "No. Mage!" Gunshots exploded, deafening him. He cringed, expecting the impact of a slug, but none came.

Hughes cursed.

Another shot rang out. Mage rolled over in time to see Hughes make a dash for the tunnel. He disappeared around the corner. Seconds later, a terrified scream cut through the silence, then ended abruptly.

Mage stared in disbelief at the dark tunnel.

Chapter Twenty-three

They lost no time in pulling out of the cave, the wagon loaded with chattering, jubilant children. Joe led the way through the forest. Mage and the Brewster brothers rode alongside the wagon.

Rachel smiled up at Mage. "I hate to see anyone die, but I feel like a hundred pounds has been lifted from my shoulders."

With a brief nod, Mage agreed.

"I can't wait to get to the Brewster place," she added, her voice bright and cheerful. "All of the children need a bath. I could use one too."

Laura Barton nodded. "I feel like a walking cake of dirt."

Mage's thoughts drifted away from the women's animated conversation. He couldn't help thinking about the cord across the mouth of the tunnel back in the cave.

Hughes had deliberately set it? Why? To keep one of the women or children from slipping away? He didn't think so. The idea that Joe had plunged to his death in the tunnel would have been more than enough to prevent anyone venturing back into the depths of the cave.

Ahead, Mage spotted the windfall under which he and William had spent the night. He shook his head. That seemed like a month ago, and he couldn't remember the last time he wasn't surrounded by children.

Without warning, his hat flew off his head at the same time the crack of a rifle shot shattered the silent forest. Mage threw himself from the saddle and remained motionless. He braced for another shot, but none came.

Rachel screamed. The horses squealed and thrashed about.

A guttural voice overpowered the commotion. "Don't nobody move, or I'll put a chunk of lead in them."

Mage stiffened at the voice.

Shank Hughes!

Before he had time to wonder how the rustler managed to pull it all off, he heard footsteps in the rain-soaked leaves coming in his direction.

"That's right. Don't nobody move 'til I make certain that schoolteacher got what he deserved."

Through slit eyes, Mage watched Hughes draw closer. He cursed himself for not thinking fast enough to grab his Colt before hitting the ground. He remained motionless.

Hughes halted at Mage's side. The click of a hammer being cocked sounded like a cannon.

Rachel screamed. "No!"

Mage kicked his foot forward, catching Hughes behind the knees and knocking his legs from under him. In the next instant, he leaped on the fallen outlaw, seizing his gun hand with a grip of steel.

Hughes cursed and swung his free hand, catching Mage on the jaw and knocking his head back, but the gambler clung desperately to the hand holding the sixgun. They rolled over and came to a halt against a pine. Mage slammed Hughes' gun hand into the pine, sending the revolver spinning several feet into the leaves near the wagon.

Leaping to his feet, Mage grabbed for his Colt, but in the struggle, it had fallen from the holster. Cursing, Hughes jumped at him, fastening his thick fingers around Mage's neck.

Mage pummeled the rustler's stomach with short, driving blows, but it was like pounding a sheet of iron. Pressure began building in Mage's ears. A burst of red filled his eyes.

Mustering all his strength, he slammed the edge of his hand across the bridge of Shank's nose.

"Yaaa," the rustler screamed and jerked his hands to his broken nose.

Gasping for breath, Mage stumbled back. From the corner of his eye, he spotted the sunlight reflect from the barrel of his revolver lying half-covered by leaves.

He stepped forward, driving a looping right into Hughes' bearded jaw. The force of the blow spun Hughes' head. Mage threw a left hook that spun the rustler's head in the other direction, sending him spinning up against the scaly bark of an ancient loblolly pine.

Mage waded in, well aware that the worst mistake a fighter could make was not to follow up on his advantage.

Hughes surprised him. Before Mage could deliver a follow up blow, the rustler bounced off the tree and threw a straight right that just brushed Mage's jaw. Mage jabbed the larger man twice, then lowered his shoulder and whipped a half hook, half uppercut at Hughes' jaw.

The blow spun the rustler around, and Mage charged,

looping another right. The rustler ducked and lunged forward, driving his shoulder into Mage's stomach and propelling him back into the wagon wheel.

A cry of pain burst from Mage's lips as the back of his head bounced off the iron tire. For a moment, the excruciating pain paralyzed him. Hughes stepped back and drove a knotted fist into the middle of Mage's chest, aggravating the pain.

Waves of searing fire washed over him, but Mage threw his arms around Hughes' head and wrestled him to the ground. Flailing at each other, they rolled under the wagon. Hughes ended on top, pummeling Mage's face. Mage managed to grab a handful of the rustler's greasy black hair and clenching his teeth, slammed Hughes' head into the wagon bed.

The horses, frightened by the gunshots and fighting, lunged forward, catching Hughes in the back with the bolster of the wagon.

He screamed as the impact flung him forward.

Before Mage could move, a rear wheel ran over his outstretched hand. Bones popped like dead branches.

He cradled his right hand to his chest and staggered to his feet. Legs spread, shoulders hunched against the pain, he stared at the rustler who struggled to his feet. For several seconds, the two stood glaring at each other.

"I figured you was dead," Mage gasped out.

A sneer played over Hughes' thin lips. "You ain't the only smart one, schoolteacher. I knew that old man would bring you back."

Now, everything in the cave made sense to Mage, even the cord stretched across the mouth of the tunnel. "You deliberately let Joe escape."

"It worked."

"And you faked your own death."

"Then hightailed it right out the back, just like your old man over there." His black eyes glittered when they lit on Mage's crippled hand, then focused on the holster on Mage's right hip. "Too bad about that hand, schoolteacher. Looks like you drew to an inside straight and missed. You got no hold-out now," he added, referring to the absent Derringer.

A hundred yards up the trail, Rachel managed to rein in the frightened horses. She stood in the wagon and looked back.

Mage waved for her to stay put with the children. He spoke to Hughes. "Sometimes you hit it, sometimes you don't."

Hughes' sneer spread across his weathered face. Without warning, the rustler leaped for his revolver which lay half hidden in the leaves.

Mage threw himself backward, scrabbling for his own revolver.

A shot rang out. Dirt and leaves exploded in Mage's face. His left fingers touched the butt of his Colt. Coolly and calmly, he twisted around as another shot echoed through the forest. A burning sensation ripped along his side.

In less than a second, Mage's hand blurred as he fanned the hammer three times. The three shots sounded as one.

Hughes' eyes widened in surprise. His jaw dropped. For a few seconds, he remained motionless, and then he dropped to his knees. Slowly his gaze shifted to the Colt in Mage's left hand. He tried to speak, but no words came.

Mage answered the unspoken question Hughes tried to ask. "Just because I wear my holster on my right doesn't mean I can't shoot with my left."

Hughes' eyes rolled up in his head, and he tumbled over on his side.

* * *

Mage sat beside Rachel as she pointed the wagon toward the Brewster ranch. His side burned where the slug grazed him. His fingers throbbed, and he knew he was due for a heap more hurt when Doc Shelby set his broken bones.

The dun trailed behind the wagon, Shank Hughes draped over the saddle.

"Looks like your teaching days are about over," she said, keeping her eyes forward.

Mage glanced at her. The light breeze tousled her black hair. "Looks that way. Of course, we still got the kids to look after until their folks get back."

She shrugged. "I reckon you're getting tired of kids about now." There was an edge to her voice, half-wistful, half-hopeful.

Mage peered to the west, toward California. Somehow, it had lost some of its appeal. He looked at Rachel again. "I don't know. I reckon I'm getting used to them. What do you reckon that means?"

A glimmer of hope filled her eyes. "I–I don't know. What do you think?"

A flush of color burned his cheeks. For a moment, he couldn't speak, but he finally managed to croak out. "I figure it means I ought to settle down and have some youngsters of my own. What do you think?"

Tears glittered in her eyes when she smiled up at him. "I think you're right."

Behind them in the wagon, Laura Barton and the girls giggled.